The Hunted

Part 1

Being the pets of wealthy, seductive, and successful Vampires has its benefit. Until their centuries-old enemies begin to hunt you down as well

Ayna Dix

Table of Contents

Prologue

"Hurry! Hide, Sister Carmel!" A girl of 21 years old screamed as she took the older woman's blood-stained hand and ran to the barn. The ducks and chickens scrambled out of their way, their bare, muddy feet leading them to what they hoped was safety. The bells tolled. The screams filled the air. The Norsemen had arrived. The day had been unassuming. The girl had gone to Morning Prayer, completed her work, and prepared their evening meal. In the girl's 11 years at the convent, rarely had a day been any different.

The girl had turned to the convent when she had run away from her kidnappers. She had been walking in the woods, a girl of merely 10 when the men had stumbled upon her. Silencing her screams, they had gaged and thrown her into the back of their cart. She only escaped when the soldiers came past, using them as a distraction as she ran back into the woods. She ran for what had felt like hours and eventually knocked on the doors of the convent. She had been under the protection of the Sisters ever since.

"In here," the girl urgently said, crouching down next to a pile of firewood as a tall, strong, voluptuous woman wielding an ax strode into the barn. The girl had never seen a woman look so formidable.

"My my, what do we have here," the Norsewoman mocked as she grabbed Sister Carmel's wrist and pulled her up, slicing her ax through Sister Carmel's neck before the girl could register what was happening. Standing up, the girl smiled, a smile she wasn't sure why she was expressing. She had taken the tall Norsewoman by surprise. The wicked grin on her face sent a shiver down the girl's spine. Taking her cloth robe off, the girl stood in front of the Norsewoman, naked and amidst the chaos of the day, feeling free for the first time in her life.

"Take me," the girl said, the Norsewoman raising her eyebrow. She circled the girl, grabbing at her flesh and smelling her, kissing her neck.

"I think I will," the Norsewoman said, grabbing the girl's wrist and walking her out back into the moonlight. The girl had thought it strange that the Norsemen would come at night. Usually, they preferred the day, but as the strong, seductive Norsewoman protected her young naked, vulnerable body by a mere look directed toward any man who tried to approach her, the girl knew that her questions could wait.

"What's your name," the Norsewoman said, sitting the girl in her longboat and draping an animal skin over her shoulders. The Norsewoman was older than the girl, her fiery, long red hair braided. Her piercing green eyes were highlighted by the dark powdered shadow band around her eyes. The markings on the Norsewoman's upper arms, making her look even fiercer as her biceps flexed, the girl feeling herself have unnatural thoughts and making her shiver as the Norsewoman ran her hands over her body.

"What are you doing?" The girl softly asked, involuntarily moaning as the Norsewoman ran her hands in between her thighs, spreading them slightly. Running her hands up her thighs and toward the girl's thick bush of pubic hair, her thumbs spreading the girl's pussy lips slightly and noticing her slick wetness. The Norsewoman looked up at the girl, matching the desire in her eyes and biting her bottom lip seductively.

"You truly are a demon," the girl said, trying to push the Norsewoman away but making her laugh.

"Yes, my sweet girl, I am. Yet, I am a demon who will love you until the end of time," the Norsewoman said, tucking a strand of the girl's raven black hair behind her ear and passing her a knife, the Norsewoman exposing her neck.

"I was merely checking for disease," the Norsewoman replied. The girl ran the knife down the side of the Norsewoman's neck. She was confused about the feelings which flooded her being. The girl shook her head and passed the knife back, looking up at the Norsewoman with an innocence that drove the Norsewoman wild. The Norsewoman smiled and wrapped her arm around the girl and bringing her in close, delighted that the girl did not refuse her touch and relaxed into her side. The girl looked out to the shoreline. The billowing plumes of smoke filling the sky as yells and shrieks were silenced after the sound of metal piercing flesh. The sound of the raiding party pillaging sent a shudder of terror down the girl's body, another one coming as the Norsewoman kissed the girl's cheek.

"I'm Demelza," the girl said, replying to the kiss and turning her face to the Norsewoman.

"How can you speak my language?" Demelza asked, her curious eyes looking over the

Norsewoman.

"I have many skills and gifts. In time, you might have them too," the Norsewoman replied with a laugh.

"You can call me, Uda," the Norsewoman said, introducing herself and passing Demelza a piece of bread, kissing her cheek again, making Demelza blush.

"Eat. You'll be hungry soon, now that you don't need to run for your life," Uda instructed, laying down and stroking Demelza's back as she looked up at the stars. Demelza ate as she watched the place she once called home being destroyed as she obeyed her first instruction, surprised that she held little grief in her heart.

Chapter 1

The afternoon sun belted into the restaurant's floor to ceiling windows. Nikita shifting her foot backward as she dodged its rays and sipped her red wine. She gazed to her left, noticing the man who was watching her with lustful intensity.

Oh, if only you knew, Nikita thought to herself, smiling. She turned her head toward the street, watching as the city slowly transformed from trendy urban cafes and restaurants into a wild, neon wonderland where everything was on offer for the right price. Maybe it was the salacious nature of this particular city that kept her here. Or perhaps it was the beautiful women who flocked to the place, searching for their dreams to come to fruition. But in the city of dreams, no one seemed to mention the nightmares which filled the nights. Nikita smirked to herself as she replayed her last night's exploits. She and Uda had gone out to eat, finding tasty Chinese morsels along the graffiti-covered alley outside of Chinatown. The gleam in her eye as she reminisced was unmissable as Nikita took out her leather-bound journal and pen.

The most recent time-wasting exercise I have allowed myself to indulge in is the one they now call journaling. It's had many names, but this one is my favorite. So I'm sitting here, in this place overlooking the cityscape, journaling. I've done this so many times before; I'm slightly less offended by the notion each time. I find it truly baffling that humans believe their existence is so riveting that it requires a written memoir.

My therapist said that I should try focusing on myself more, telling my truth instead of judging others. She said this to me while judging my shoes, so I don't know how reliable she'll be. She looks like a tasty snack, though, so for one reason or the next, she'll turn out to be useful. Here goes.

My name is one that invites too many questions, so I have long traded Demelza for new variants over the years, my most recent selection, Nikita. I had chosen Sophia last time I felt like reinventing myself. I must have a thing for names ending in A. As here I sit, Nikita Jones, 35 years old for the last 950 years and still as deeply in love with Uda as I have ever been. She still calls me Demelza, making me feel more seen than anything else she could ever say. My Norsewoman, my protector, my Mistress.

Nikita looked up from her journal as her alarm went off, signaling that the outside world was dark enough for her to move freely. She had managed to dodge the sun by driving into the undercover parking lot, but now she had jobs to do. Taking one final sip of wine, Nikita raised her eyebrows to the man who had locked eyes on her, making her laugh at his attempt to seduce her with his intense, almost challenging stare.

The grocery shop was the one chore that Nikita did for her girls. She often wondered why she bothered doing this for them, it wasn't like they needed her too, but over the last few decades, she had grown increasingly aware of her desire to be needed and adored. She reached for the box of cereal Hannah ate, smiling to herself as she put it in the cart, thinking about Hannah eating it while sitting on the kitchen bench, and swinging her legs. Nikita checked it off her list and continued through the store.

I wish it were this easy for me, Nikita bitterly thought, imagining a store for her particular tastes. Deciding that it was best to push that thought from her mind as she felt a girl brush past her.

"Sorry," the girl said, her white teeth flashing and making Nikita turn away.

I need to get home, Nikita said to herself,

feeling her eyes begin to change and her hunger pierced her.

Uda and Nikita had ten multimillion-dollar homes worldwide, several apartment blocks, and numerous commercial businesses, with just enough shares in various companies meaning their luxurious lifestyle could be maintained without a second thought. This was the custom for most of their kind, having more than they would ever need, but not so much that mainstream media noticed them.

The place they had called home for the last seven years was nestled deep in the woodlands, between two mountains, a river running through their land. It provided them privacy and allowed them to live undisturbed by the going ons of the city. It also meant that it was an hour's drive to the city. The time to get there was considerably less when Nikita and Uda ran through the trees at night, but far slower by car, regardless of how close to the floor Nikita pressed the acceleration pedal.

Nikita smiled as she approached the large, iron gates with the U and D in the center of each gate, waiting for them to open. Driving slower down the lavender lined driveway, Nikita passed the waterfalls on either side of the drive, coming to a stop in front of the large doors of the luxurious mansion. Getting out, she threw the keys to their valet before picking up the grocery bags taking a moment to admire her home. The mountains surrounding the property still had their snow peaks, the stars glittering across the sky, and the sound of music and laughter coming from inside the home, made her heart swell.

"Did you get the groceries?" Uda called from the couch. Nikita walked past Uda, sitting on the lounge, a 20 something-year-old draped over her, the girl's head lying on Uda's chest, and a white towel pressed to her neck. Nikita walked into the kitchen and placed the grocery bags on the bench before turning back to Uda.

"Of course," she replied, tilting her head questioningly before frowning.

"What's the occasion?" Nikita asked, walking back over to the lounge and gently taking the girl in her arms.

"Shh, it's alright, sweetheart, this will only hurt a little," Nikita whispered as she brought her mouth down, letting her fangs press into the puncture marks that Uda had left. Sucking, Nikita's eyes rolled back into her head, and she moaned in delight, stroking the girl's head as she let out a whimper, making Nikita chuckle to herself before pulling herself off the girl's neck and mopped up the spilled blood with the towel. Kissing the girl's forehead, Nikita laid her face up over her lap, stroking her stomach lazily and cradling her head in her arm.

"That was unexpected," Nikita sighed, resting her head on Uda's shoulder.

"What are we celebrating?" Nikita asked, repeating her question as Uda smirked and looked at Nikita seductively.

"They found him," Uda replied, the look in her eye telling Nikita the news she had been waiting to hear for over a decade.

"I mean, it was going to become easy at some point. He's getting old," Nikita replied. She looked down to see the girl stir in her arms, smiling down at her as she brought her up to her chest and held her tightly.

"You really shouldn't play with your food," Uda remarked, raising an eyebrow at Nikita. Nikita smirked, rocking the girl like a baby, settling her.

"But look at her," Nikita replied. Uda had chosen particularly well. The girl not only tasted divine, but her body was stirring a heat in Nikita that she knew would be demanding to be relieved before the night was through.

"They taste so much better when they want you to," Nikita replied, waiting for the girl to snuggle in close to her.

"Can I have just a little bit more?" Nikita softly asked, making her face soft and nonthreatening as she held the girl in a loving embrace. The girl subtly nodded her head as Nikita took her forearm in one hand and rolled the girl's face into her chest with the other.

"Demi, you're going to make her fall in love with you. And we have no space for another pet," Uda said, watching and waiting, rolling her eyes and getting up. Nikita loved that Uda still called her by her original name. It reminded her that they had shared the most of this world together, that no one else on the planet had more history with her than Uda. Uda walked over to the bar and took a bottle from the shelf, walking back over to Nikita and pulling her head back.

"Here. You're going to drain her if you're not careful," Uda said, pushing the bottle into Nikita's hands before taking the girl out of Nikita's arms. Nikita raised an eyebrow out of disdain but allowed Uda to take the girl out of sight and into their bedroom.

"I want to stay. I can keep going," the girl mumbled, making Uda smile at her affectionately.

"I know you can, sweetheart. I just don't want you to," Uda replied, lying to the girl. She knew fair well that the girl was pushing herself past her limits, and as much as she wanted to, Uda wasn't about to allow for that to happen. Uda stroked the girl's forehead as she fell asleep, surprising herself at the softness she felt toward her and patting her absentmindedly on her chest before she walked back out into the living room where Nikita was watching Kelsey and Nerada begin to unpack the groceries.

"Hello, Mistress," Kelsey said, coming over and kissing Uda's cheek before giving her a cheeky look and returning to the kitchen. Nerada smiled and dropped her head. She had begun ending her relationship with Nikita and Uda, and her lack of protocol was something Uda had to remind herself was acceptable.

Uda sat down next to Nikita and watched as Hannah came upstairs and began making her dinner, followed by Eden. Holly burst through the door in her usual dramatic way, and Cleo was busy drying herself off outside after spending the afternoon doing laps in the pool.

"All my pets, home at last," Uda remarked as she watched them all begin to buzz around the kitchen.

"Why do you call us that?" Eden asked. Eden was the youngest, at 21 years old, and was the newest addition to Uda and Nikita's *family*. They had picked her up when she was 20 and addicted to heroin after years on the streets, cleaned her up, and offered her a place in the family. She had been hesitant at first, wondering what the catch was, but the contract and terms of the agreement she had with Uda and Nikita were too good to pass up. So, every Monday night, she let Uda and Nikita feed on her, sampling her blood and using her as an entrée or dessert, depending on their mood.

That was the agreement Uda and Nikita had with all their girls. They gave them a luxurious lifestyle and helped them get set up with whatever endeavor their hearts desired, for the small price of weekly bloodletting. They never fed on a girl younger than 21 or older than 35, a sentimental notion toward Nikita who, at 21, met Uda, and at 35 was given the bite for her birthday, forever tying Nikita to Uda's side, forever making Uda Nikita's Mistress.

"Because my gorgeous girl, old habits die hard," Nikita said, getting up from her spot on the lounge and walking over to Eden, taking her wrist in her hand and bringing her back to the lounge.

"My pasta is going to over boil, Mistress," Eden softly said, Nikita just smiling.

"Then don't fight us, or it'll take longer," Uda replied, pulling Eden down and into her arms.

"Oh, here I was thinking we were going to have dinner together as a family," Kelsey called from the kitchen, making the other women laugh as they continued to cook. Nerada was 32 years old and the eldest in the family, taking over from

Eden and finishing her meal for her. After ten years with Uda and Nikita, she knew that Eden would need something to eat once they were through with her. Although they never drained the girls, merely taking 600ml each, it took its toll as the weeks turned into months.

Nikita ran her fingers down Eden's body, breathing her in and pulling her close as she felt her fangs protrude and sunk them into the girl's young, soft flesh. Uda pulled her from her other side, mimicking the action, and Eden shut her eyes, melting into their arms as the other women continued to cook and laugh about things that happened in their day or people they had interactions with. This was a typical night in their household. Each girl was given a particular night where she offered herself to her Mistresses, each dynamic slightly different from the next. Uda and Nikita forbid the girls from being with anyone sexually for the duration of their contracts. While they were permitted to begin dating at 31, sex was off the table. This was merely out of Uda and Nikita's preference. They didn't like sharing their girls. It also meant that they could tailor their dynamic with each girl, depending on the type of play she desired.

Eden was still getting used to being taken, although Uda and Nikita had both noticed how she loved an element of voyeurism to their sessions. Their relationship with Hannah was more nurturing and gentle, both Uda and Nikita taking on a Mommy Domme role. Hannah liked to snuggle into them every opportunity she could, and she was Nikita's favorite, as her needs challenged Nikita to embrace a softer side to her style of domination. After 950 years on earth, Nikita enjoyed anything that could still challenge her, enjoying the mental stimulation of coming up with new play scenes that didn't involve a dungeon. Kelsey was the complete opposite of Hannah. She liked it rough, enjoying denial play, deep penetration, and being fed on with force. This was why Uda had always given her special attention, her willingness to be used was in utter alignment with Uda's preferred domination style, and she loved that she could treat Kelsey like prey and have her enjoy it. Holly got off everything Kelsey did but liked to include impact play, mild pet play, and suffocation. Cleo wasn't particularly interested in sex, something that both Uda and Nikita had taken some getting used to, but managed to find a middle ground. Cleo liked to watch, and her Mistresses had no problem putting on a show for her, feeding on her as they finished. Then there was Nerada, who was coming to the end of her contract with Uda and Nikita. On her 35th birthday, she would be allowed to end her dynamic with her Mistresses and continue her human life outside of the family. Nerada had always been a sensual lover, preferring to be fed on amid a gentle orgasm, but it was the psychological power play and being a service sub that she knew she would miss the most.

"We all called our humans pets. It's just recently that *we've* started calling you our girls.

But you are just pets to most of the others in our coven. We are progressive. Like vegans were a while ago in your world. Some people get it, others not so much," Nikita said after she pulled off Eden, gasping for air.

"The others in our coven often joke about the degree to which we care for you girls because most others of our kind treat their humans with the same disregard they have been for hundreds of years. Similar to that of a standard human with their dog, hence, pets. They'll keep them clean enough, fed and exercised, but nothing else particularly special," Uda added, wiping the blood from her bottom lip. Eden moaned and placed her hands on Nikita and Uda's thighs.

"We, on the other hand, would be similar to those crazy dog ladies who let their pets sleep in their bed, put them in outfits, and treat them like their baby," Nikita added, making Cleo laugh.

"Yes, that's right, you're my little bitch," Uda said, directing her comment toward Holly, making her giggle.

"Do you like it when the other girls watch you?" Nikita softly asked, directing her attention back to Eden's body, feeling the heat from deep within her. Eden looked up, the fear of her secret being found out, making her blush.

"We know it turns you on," Uda whispered, placing her hand between Eden's thighs and spreading her legs. Holly looked over to where they were, raising an eyebrow as she nudged Hannah, who just smirked and began watching as well.

"Look, they are all watching you. They want to see you perform for them. Let's put on a show," Nikita seductively said, running her fingers under Eden's t-shirt, liking that Eden hadn't bothered to put on a bra and began stroking her breasts, making her nipples hard before biting back down on her. Hannah put the finishing touches on her meal before she came to the opposite lounge and joined Holly and Nerada. They were already there, Kelsey and

Cleo joining them as well as they watched Eden being sensually toyed with as she offered her body up to her Mistresses. Smirking, Uda stood Eden up and made her sit on her lap, facing the other women as she reached around the front of her t-shirt, ripping it down the middle and exposing her body, giving her goosebumps. Nikita noticed the slightest withdrawal from Eden, looking at Uda.

That took her close to her limit, Nikita said to Uda telepathically, Uda nodding her head and placing her hand on Eden's throat, her other hand on her pussy making her gasp just as Uda roughly brought her mouth down, making Eden let out a pained exhale.

"Shh. You're not done satisfying us yet," Nikita said, sinking her fangs into Eden's inner thigh, making her howl before she stopped and licked her lips. Uda wrapped Eden in her arms as Nikita walked over to where her pasta dish had been made by Nerada, coming back with it and carefully placing it in Uda's hand. Uda's other arm was wrapped around Eden, who had curled into the embrace.

"Here, sweetie," Nikita said, as the other girls slowly lost interest and began talking amongst themselves.

"Movie?" Holly asked, the others beginning to discuss what sort of film they would or wouldn't be interested in watching. Uda gently fed Eden, her weary body laying limp in Uda's arms as Nikita opened her arms to Hannah, who bounded into them, falling back onto the lounge with her. Her blanket in tow, Hannah kissed Nikita, feeling her hands on her body, making her arch her back.

"Hi, baby girl, Mommy's missed you," Nikita whispered, breaking the kiss, making Hannah happy as she rested her face against Nikita's generous breast. Nikita held her tight, placing her hand on Hannah's cheek and holding her face to her breast, feeling Hannah melt into her and beginning to play with her diamond necklace as the other women continued to debate which movie would be acceptable.

It was after midnight by the time the movie had ended. They had decided on an action film that seemed never to end, yet when it did, they threw popcorn at the screen, annoyed at the weak story plot. Hannah had fallen asleep in Nikita's arms, Nikita having placed her gently in her bed and tucking her in before finding Uda, sitting on the upper deck of their bedroom, overlooking the ocean. Their house was in a marvelous location. One side was the ocean, the other side mountains.

"So, you still haven't told me what the plan is," Nikita asked as she sat next to Uda, placing her legs over the top of Uda's and wrapping her arms around hers.

"They found him by Jackson's Lake. Apparently, he hadn't eaten in days and was paranoid," Uda began to explain. Like all supernatural beings, their coven and many others were constantly under attack from those determined to wipe out their kind. This man had been no different, just more successful. But while Vampire Hunters were always at their heels, the Vampires had their own warriors, equally as determined to preserve their kind. These warriors fought under the Vampire governing body, The Order. An old profession that had aided in Vampires' survival for as long as time had been recorded.

"So, why do I feel as though it has not been just an easy grip and rip?" Nikita asked, wondering why this had made the news. Usually, when The Order had found a Hunter, they simply tore them apart and left them in the desert.

"They want to make an example of him. Firstly, never has a Hunter lived this long, and secondly, killed so many of our kind. The other Hunters look to him as their leader. The Order want to make a show of what happens when we find them," Uda explained. She and Nikita had both been warriors of The Order, leaving after their mandatory 400 years of service.

"I would have loved to have hunted him. I thought that he would have died in the fire. I still remember his wife. She was something," Nikita said as she watched wave after wave crash against the rocks.

"You caught some pretty impressive ones," Uda replied, smiling up at the moon and cracking her neck.

"They want everyone there," Uda added. This was the part that she was holding off telling Nikita as she loved her girls and hated leaving them. However, when The Order demanded an audience, it would prove to be detrimental not to show.

"When, for how long?" Nikita nearly whined. She hated being summoned.

"What is the point of being all of this if I still have to do what I'm told?" Nikita complained, making Uda laugh.

"It is just meant to be a weekend. We might stay longer if it's fun. It would be good to catch up with everyone. And no, we're not taking them," Uda quickly added, hearing Nikita's next thought.

"It was just a question," Nikita laughed, hoping that it would be a simple weekend trip. Family reunions with their coven always ended with various members either not speaking to each other or a death or two. Their coven was prone to drama.

Chapter 2

The weekends and weekdays were more or less the same within the household, with only 3 of the girls having standard 9-5 jobs. Holly was a Vet, Cleo worked at an art gallery in the city, and Nerada taught the 4th grade at a local school.

"Girls' your lunch is on the kitchen bench," Nikita called out as she walked through the house after writing cute post-it notes and placing them on each of their containers. Nerada just smirked, took the sticky notes off her lunch and snacks, and put them in her diary before packing everything into her handbag.

"Thank you, Mistress," Nerada said, knowing that it would hurt like hell to leave the family in a few years' time, leaning in and passionately kissing Nikita before she walked out the door. Cleo was next to leave, just as Nikita saw Hannah run through the trees of the forest, which circled their home, jogging up to the back glass doors and laying down, spent.

"I'll be home a little later tonight, Mistress. There's a buyer who is coming in to look at the new pieces we have, and he's apparently really important so, I have to stay later," Cleo bitterly said, making Nikita smile.

"Do you want me in the area in case he tries something?" She asked, pulling Cleo to her and running her hands down her back as she held her. Cleo melted into the embrace, resting her head on Nikita's shoulder.

"No, I think I'll be alright. Another girl is staying behind as well," Cleo replied, standing back up and smiling at Nikita before leaving. Kelsey sleepily walked upstairs, followed closely by Uda.

"You weren't as quiet as you thought," Nikita laughed, referring to Uda's vain attempt to mask her moans as she had let Kelsey fuck her.

"Well, maybe I was inviting you to join us,

but you were too busy playing domestic goddess," Uda replied, wrapping her arms around Nikita and kissing her passionately as Hannah walked into the kitchen.

"Good morning," Hannah exaggeratedly said, looking at Kelsey's exhausted face making her laugh.

"Don't even," Kelsey replied, the smile on her face and her shaking head, making Hannah roll her eyes playfully. The girls had long learned that when their Mistresses had a need that required filling, it got filled. Kelsey wearily pulled herself on top of the kitchen bench, her eyes expressing her gratitude as Uda pushed a bowl of cereal into her hands.

"Eat up. We aren't done yet," Uda said, patting the side of Kelsey's thigh.

"Oh fuck," Kelsey defeatedly mumbled as she spooned a mouthful of cereal into her mouth, making Uda smirk.

"I like making them their lunches," Nikita replied, taking out a bag from the fridge and ripping it open with her teeth as Holly walked up the stairs, talking loudly on the phone.

"Thank you, Mistress," Holly quietly said, placing her phone to her breasts as she kissed Nikita before reaching for her bag, finding Uda pressing into her.

"You forgot this," Uda whispered, sucking on a pink butt plug before quickly pulling out the back of Holly's pants and making her spread her thighs. Uda pushed it in slowly, smirking as she felt Holly give in as she spoke on the phone down about a dog that needed an operation that day. Holly had always been the most dramatic one they had kept, often finding herself in situations where she required Uda or Nikita is rescue her. They had found Holly by chance. They had been drinking in the bar that she had previously worked for, and Nikita and Uda had shamelessly flirted with her, as did most of the other patrons. The difference was, Uda would almost routinely find herself protecting Holly from one creepy guy or the next. With full DD breasts, a thin waist, and thick thighs complimenting her flowing honey blonde hair and big blue eyes, she was hard to miss. Holly had been more than receptive toward Uda and Nikita, refusing to let them pay for their drinks and often drinking with them as the night turned into the early morning.

"You know, if you wanted to, I could walk you home. It's dangerous for two gorgeous women to be walking alone at this hour, regardless of how bright the moon is outside," Holly had boldly said, wiping down the bench and walking around to the front of the bar. Nikita had erupted in laughter at the notion that Holly could protect them, making Holly blush.

"Oh, sweetie, I'm not laughing at you. You're just so sweet, I'm not sure you'd be able to," Nikita laughed, becoming very serious when Holly placed her hands on Uda's thighs as she sat on a barstool.

"I'm not that sweet," she said, leaning forward and kissing Uda on the lips, making Nikita's eyes grow wide as Uda held her hand out.

"I can see that," Nikita said, taking Uda's hand and enclosing Holly from behind, pushing into her ass and moaning as her hands reached around to her front, ripping her blouse open.

"We aren't either," Uda smugly remarked, seeing Holly's surprise at Nikita's groping hands. Uda spread her thighs and pushed herself to the edge of the stool. Took Holly's face in her hands and kissed her softly, feeling for Holly's tongue, smiling when Holly offered it to her without Uda having to ask.

"If you come home with us, we might never let you leave," Nikita teased, running her hand up the back of Holly's head and grabbing a fistful of hair before slowly bringing it back until her eyes met Nikita's. Holly had just smiled, feeling Uda kiss down her body.

"I wouldn't want to be anywhere else," Holly replied the surrender in her voice, the increase of her pulse, exciting Uda.

"So, what are you up to?" Eden said, hovering in Kelsey's doorway. Kelsey took her earphones from her ears and smiled at Eden. Kelsey had built a successful online business creating motivational YouTube videos. It took her two years of consistent work, often working when the other girls played in the pool or watched movies together. At 4 in the morning, she got up early, meditated, watched some content from her favorite creators, and got in 3 hours of work before she had breakfast. Hannah had modeled her daily routine after seeing how much of the day Kelsey was able to harness. However, Hannah had decided to be a freelance writer. The work was more profitable in the short term. So once Hannah built a reputation for herself and was pulling in just over $10,000 a month, she just rinsed and repeated the process. Kelsey, on the other hand, wanted more.

"Working," she replied, finding Eden's eye roll amusing. Eden walked into her room and sat on her bed, crossing her legs.

"Yeah, I get that, but it's 3:30, and everyone will be home soon, and I'm so bored. I've shopped for everything that I could ever want, worked out, and had every treatment I could want. What do I even do now?" Eden explained. It was true. The first year or so with Uda and Nikita was the best thing that anyone could ever imagine. Their unlimited cash poured into the girls' hands like flowing water from a freshly tapped well. All of their wildest dreams were realized until the thrill of buying a $5,000 wallet no longer held any joy. The parties became boring and dull. They learned that their friends were only in the friendship for what they could scavenge, and there were only so many gadgets on the market. Kelsey looked at Eden and turned her chair around.

"Well, now you're ready to start living. Your last year was just a dream. That's why it felt so fucking good. But it wasn't real. Don't worry, we all did it. How can you not when they hand you access to everything you've ever dreamed of?

However, now that you have and know that you can have everything you want, you can focus on doing something you want. Just don't forget, one day you'll be on your own again. You don't want to have all this cool stuff and no cash flow coming in. You'll want to think of something you can do that'll bring you in an income before you're on your own," Kelsey explained. She liked that Kelsey didn't make her feel bad for her extravagant shopping sprees. Eden thought for a moment before smiling at Kelsey.

"Thanks," she said as she heard Nerada's voice in the living room and leaving to let Kelsey finish her work.

"Hi," Eden said, walking into the room to see Nerada blushing on the phone. She pulled a face and walked to the fridge and took out an apple, going to sit on the couch and wait for Nerada to get off the phone.

"I'm not telling you that!" Nerada exclaimed, eyeing Eden playfully and rolling her eyes.

"I have to go, bye," Nerada said, hanging up the phone and sighing as she put it in her skirt pocket.

"Hey," she sighed, opening the fridge and taking out the slice of cake she had been saving.

"Who was that?" Eden inquisitively asked the smirk that came on Nerada's face piquing her curiosity.

"So, when you turn 31, you can start dating. And so, that was this guy that I'm talking to at the moment," Nerada explained as Uda came into the room.

"Oh god, keep it in your pants. I don't need to hear those thoughts," she said, making Nerada laugh and bite her bottom lip.

"Tell me all about him in the hot tub?" Eden asked, Nerada thinking about the papers she had to grade, deciding they could wait as she nodded her head and stood up excitedly. Uda smiled to herself, secretly happy that in their time keeping the girls, not once had anyone been jealous of the other.

"I know, we are lucky," Nikita said out loud, replying to Uda's thoughts, coming behind her and kissing her cheek.

"I love you," Nikita whispered, hearing the door unlock, and Holly burst through the door in her usual dramatic way.

"You would not believe the day I've had," Holly loudly said to no one in particular, both Uda and Nikita peeping behind the kitchen wall.

"Oh, hi, Mistresses," Holly said, switching to a different side of her personality, placing her bag down slowly to not make too much noise, and quickly walking outside to join Eden and Nerada.

"Fuck me. I think I just interrupted something!" Holly exclaimed, seeing Nerada and Eden sitting in the hot tub. Nerada turned around and abruptly stopped talking.

"Yeah, you've got a habit of that," she remarked, slightly annoyed.

"Nerada has a boyfriend," Eden said, getting splashed with warm water from Nerada.

"You're such a child," Holly laughed, stripping naked and joining them in the tub.

"So, do share," she said, easing herself down and feeling the stress of the day begin to wash away.

"He is tall, tanned, brown hair and blue eyes," Nerada gushed, blushing as she remembered how his toothy, cheeky grin made her heart skip a beat.

"He sounds awful," Hannah bitterly said, walking past them and rolling her eyes as she went inside to shower after finishing her session with her personal trainer.

"What's with her?" Eden asked, surprised that Hannah was so hot and cold. Nerada just smirked.

"Who knows, maybe she just needs a cuddle," Nerada said, turning back to Eden and Holly and continuing their conversation.

***

Zagan opened the door to his truck and jumped out. Following the same path toward the big house as his Grandfather and Father had walked before him. He thought back to Nerada, how clueless and stupid she was, living with what he and the other Hunters believed to be Vampires.

How can a teacher be so idiotic? He thought to himself, rolling his eyes and knocking on the door.

"Zagan, we have been expecting you," an old man with scars up and down his arms said upon opening the door. Zagan walked behind the man into a large room that had been converted into a library. Looking around, he knew that he needed to deliver some answers. He had spent months gaining Nerada's trust, enjoying everything she had offered him, but from the looks on the faces of the older men sitting around the room, he knew that his days of fun were numbered.

"Zagan, give us an update. It's been months since you've given us any information we could use, and I don't need to remind you that this is not some little cunt hunt you are going on," one man said, eyeing Zagan suspiciously. The older man could be forgiven for thinking that Zagan was only interested in getting as much from Nerada as he could without holding up his end of the bargain. He had a history of letting Vampires slip away after he had had some fun. Zagan cleared his throat and rocked on his heels.

"Well now, there is no need for such language," Zagan teased, making the older man cross his arms.

"They are going paintballing this weekend. I say, we show up and make our presence known," Zagan instructed confidently. The other men in the room murmured, causing Zagan to fear that his plan was not well received. He had always felt he had a lot to prove. He had come from a proud line of Hunters, and although his Father had trained all his brothers and one sister, Ursula, it was only he who continued the family tradition. His brothers had been killed, picked off one by one by the Vampire covens they had hunted, and his sister had fallen in love with one. That had been particularly hard on his Father, who hunted his daughter's lover for years, finally killing her in front of Ursula. That had been the day that Ursula had left the family, refusing to contact him or their Father ever again.

"It's not a bad plan. They are less likely to attack us out in the open because they would have too much of a clean-up. From everything that we have gathered on them, they seem to lead a fairly peaceful life," one of the elders explained.

"Find out the specific details. It might be a good idea for you to take her somewhere for the night so that she has someone to turn to when her whole world gets turned upside down," the elder continued, a cruel gleam in his eye. Zagan just smirked and looked to the ground.

"I don't just want to sit by and pretend to

be the good guy. I want to hunt them, I want to kill them," Zagan said, annoyed that his playboy looks had so far kept him from the action on the front line.

"Oh, you will have your chance. But right now, you need to keep close to Nerada. She is the key that will get us closer to not only Uda and Nikita, or whatever she is calling herself these days. But also the other Vampires who they turn to when we initiate the first attack. Everything we have learned about their kind is that they return to a central location when a threat appears. That is what we are waiting for, and that is when you can take up the sword," a man who was sitting at the back of the room said, standing up, followed quickly by every other Hunter in the room. The man straightened his blazer, took hold of his brass handled walking stick, and began to exit the room, placing his hand on Zagan's shoulder as he passed.

"Your Father would be proud," he said before continuing out the door, leaving Zagan standing in the room alone.

Chapter 3

"Hi beautiful," Nikita said, walking into Hannah's room, closing the door behind her. Hannah was sitting at her desk, the fire in her fireplace crackling and warming the room as the first of the winter snow feathered the ground outside her window. Hannah turned around, surprised to see Nikita leaning against the back of her door, a hot chocolate in her favorite mug in her hand.

"Oh, I just thought you might like some. I know how hard you've been working lately. I thought maybe you'd like a break? You hardly spoke at dinner, are you alright?" Nikita asked, offering the mug to Hannah. Hannah cracked her neck, sighed, and stretched before nodding her head and slowly standing up, taking her glasses off and pushing up the sleeves of her cream, cable knit sweater.

"Thank you," Hannah softly said, clearing her throat after not speaking aloud for hours, thanking Nikita once more, this time more audibly.

"It's just been a really long few days, I've got these deadlines I'm hardly reaching, and everything just feels so overwhelming," Hannah replied, smirking when Nikita pulled Hannah to her.

"Here I was thinking you were just here to keep me company," Hannah teased, making Nikita shrug her shoulder.

"Is it so bad that I tried?" Nikita replied, accepting that Hannah wasn't in the mood. Hannah walked over to the lounge, which looked out toward the forest, pulling the heavy navy curtains back and sitting down, sipping her hot chocolate and watching the snowfall.

"Your favorite time of year," Hannah said, inviting Nikita to sit next to her, her eyes smiling as Nikita walked toward her.

"Yes, no one asks why I am so cold,"

Nikita laughed, pulling a blanket from the end of the lounge and wrapped it around herself. She opened her arms to Hannah, smiling as she snuggled in close, her hot chocolate resting close to Nikita's chest as she cuddled her.

"It'll get cold if you rest it against me," Nikita whispered as she began to rock Hannah in her arms. Hannah sighed, feeling her working mindset shift as Nikita held her close, stroking her back. She sipped her hot chocolate, finishing it off quickly as it cooled, placing the mug down on the floor.

"Have you ever seen bears out here?" Hannah asked, feeling Nikita's thumbs stroking her and her biceps flex against her body.

"A few years ago, we did. But not for a few years. Maybe they'll come back this year. You'll still need to be careful if you go out into the woods," Nikita replied. She felt Hannah's mood shift, becoming sleepy as the warm liquid filled her stomach.

"Can I get you ready for bed tonight?"

Nikita whispered, making Hannah blush.

"I'm not really in the mood," Hannah replied, looking up at Nikita, worried that she'd not take no for an answer.

"I'm not that kind of monster," Nikita joked, feeling Hannah's fear, relieved when she smiled and relaxed.

"The others would think I was such a freak if they found out. I keep being scared they'll find out," Hannah confessed, Nikita, listening intently.

"Everyone has something they don't want people to know about them. You know what every other girl gets turned on by, what makes them tick, do you think they haven't figured out what yours is? Especially when you call me Mommy and not Mistress?" Nikita replied, making Hannah blush.

"You can't be too embarrassed about wanting to be loved and looked after. That's the sweetest thing we do! You've seen us suspend Holly and Kelsey overhead and force fucked them, gaged, bounded, caned, whipped, and used until they've called red, and you're worried about them laughing at you for wanting a gentle touch?" Nikita laughed, finding Hannah's fear endearing, watching as she just nodded her head.

"Well, how about this. If they ever laugh at you, and I mean really laugh at you, Mommy will just eat them," Nikita said, feeling Hannah snuggle further into her.

"Oh, I thought you told Mommy you weren't feeling it?" Nikita teased, having known all along that Hannah would submit to her.

"I wasn't then. I am now," Hannah said, reaching for Nikita's necklace, playing with it as Nikita repositioned her on her lap.

"Mommy's pretty girl," Nikita whispered, standing up and holding Hannah to her as she carried her over to her bed, laying her down gently and beginning to take her clothes off.

"I can do it," Hannah said, finding Nikita push an adult-sized pacifier into Hannah's mouth, enjoying how wide her eyes became.

"Mommy didn't ask if you could," she simply said, running her fingers over Hannah's body, giving her goosebumps.

"Lift up for Mommy," Nikita said, undressing Hannah and reaching for her pajamas.

"Such a sweet girl," Nikita said, pulling on Hannah's pajamas and kissing both of her cheeks before pulling her bedsheets down.

"Mommy," Hannah happily sighed. Nikita positioned Hannah over her lap, ripping her blouse open and pulling Hannah up and onto her nipple, moaning and putting her head back as Hannah began to suckle.

"I probably should have made you clean your teeth before bed. I guess I'm not a very good Mommy," Nikita said, thinking thoughtfully.

"No, Mommy, you're the best," Hannah said, taking Nikita's breast in her hands and her nipple from her mouth. Nikita smiled, pushing it back between her lips.

"Shh, go to sleep now, sweetheart,

Mommy, will stay with you until you fall asleep," Nikita replied, feeling Hannah's grabby hands on her breasts, and she held her.

"Have you put the baby to bed?" Uda said without looking up from her tablet. She had started a fire, turned the lights down, and drawn the curtains back from the windows. The outside lights illuminated the edge of the forest and fresh snow, creating a postcard scene.

"Yes, I have," Nikita replied, walking toward Uda but deciding to stop, standing in the vast living room, looking out of place. Uda raised an eyebrow, turned to see Nikita standing naked, her clothes strewn over the floor, her hair freshly tossed.

"Take me," Nikita softly said. Re-enacting the day she met Uda was still, after 950 years, her favorite role play. Uda smirked, putting her tablet down, never one to deny such a request.

"I think I will," Uda said, grabbing Nikita's wrist and walking her out the back doors into the moonlight, the snow falling on their faces.

"What's your name," Uda said, sitting Nikita on their outdoor lounge and draping the animal skin she had grabbed on the way out there over Nikita's shoulders. Uda untied her fiery, long red hair, quickly braiding it as her eyes looked directly into Nikita's soul. Her piercing green eyes highlighted by the seductive smokey eye that she hadn't washed off. The tattoos on Uda's upper arms made her look even fiercer as her biceps flexed. Nikita enjoyed feeling her very natural thoughts, making her shiver as Uda her hands over her body.

"What are you doing?" Nikita softly asked, moaning as Uda ran her hands in between her thighs, spreading them slightly. Running her hands up Nikita's thighs and toward the strip of pubic hair, her thumbs spreading Nikita's pussy lips slightly and noticing her slick wetness. Uda looked up at Nikita, matching the desire in her eyes as she stuck out her tongue and forcefully licked up Nikita slit seductively.

"You truly are a demon," Nikita laughed, trying to push Uda away but making her also laugh.

"Yes, my sweet girl, I am. Yet, I am a demon who will love you until the end of time," Uda breathlessly said, tucking a strand of Nikita's raven black hair behind her ear.

"I was merely checking for disease," Uda innocently replied, kissing Nikita on the cheek.

"I'm Demelza," Nikita replied, turning her face toward Uda.

"How can you speak my language?" Nikita asked.

"I have many skills and gifts. In time, you might have them too," Uda replied with a laugh, beginning to undress Nikita.

"You can call me, Uda," Uda whispered as she kissed along Nikita's neck, her fingers running through her hair.

"Oh Demelza, you will always be my only reason for living," Uda gasped as Nikita turned her on her back, straddling her waist and bringing her mouth down onto Uda's.

Chapter 4

"This is such fucking bullshit," Holly yelled as she flung her handbag down on the kitchen bench and began pouring herself a drink. She let her hair down, kicked off her shoes and socks, shaking her head as she angrily drank. It was Friday night, and the house was silent, piquing her curiosity.

"What is?" Uda said, appearing at the back door, her bikini making Holly have to swallow hard.

"Mistress," Holly gasped, feeling Uda's hands beginning to undress her. Holly was in the process of opening her practice.

"Just the design of the practice that the builders sent back to me today, they are all wrong, Mistress," Holly replied, feeling a collar being placed around her neck, Uda tightening it one hole too tight. Feeling Holly's surrender,

Uda smiled and clipped a chain leash onto the collar, leading Holly toward the hot tub where Nikita was waiting for them.

"We can fix that later. Right now, I want to put my attention somewhere else. Somewhere like this," Nikita said, reaching out of the tub and grabbing Holly's left breast, squeezing her roughly until she gasped.

"Get in here," Nikita said, taking the leash from Uda and pulling Holly in, still wearing her pants and bra. The water was warm as Holly obeyed, the heat from the water, the alcohol in her veins, and the tightening of her windpipe, all making her dizzy. This was better than she had thought it would be when she had planned this evening with Nikita and Uda.

"Mistress, I," Holly began to say, Nikita, slapping her face, silencing her.

"I don't care what you have to say," Nikita whispered, settling Holly on her lap as Uda began to flog her back, the water adding a stinging touch. Holly closed her eyes as she sighed, relaxing on Nikita's breasts and feeling Uda stop only to cuff her wrists behind her back before she continued to make her back red.

"Did you think you could submit all these lovely things, and we wouldn't explore all of them," Uda said, as she pulled Holly's pants and panties down, roughly spreading her thighs and spitting on her hand. She rubbed Holly, making her squirm as she stood legs splayed over Nikita's lap. Nikita had taken to biting into Holly's breasts, not hard enough to draw blood, but hard enough to make Holly roll her eyes back into her head. Uda had made quick work of fastening the strap on to her waist and held Holly in place as she pushed it aggressively into her without warning, smirking as she felt Holly try to deny her.

"Oh, did you think you had a choice? I'll fuck you whenever I want to. Your body belongs to me," Uda said, pounding into Holly and pulling her hair back in a fist. Nikita reached behind her, taking a gag and pushing it into

Holly's mouth, securing it behind Holly's head.

"I'm not interested in hearing you," Nikita plainly remarked, running her nails deeply down Holly's breasts, over her nipples, and down her body as Uda forced Holly's first orgasm as tears began to stream down her face.

"Is this what you needed? You needed to be used and reminded of how fucking worthless you are?" Uda questioned, feeling Holly's body become limp. Pulling out, Uda pressed the tip into Holly's ass, stretching her before she knew what was happening.

"Why are you trying to fight this? You know you are just our fuckdoll," Nikita said, replacing her fist inside of Holly and pounding her as Uda pressed further into her ass. Smiling up at Uda, Nikita opened her mouth and brought it down on Holly's neck as she fisted her forcefully, Holly beginning to rock her hips in time with Nikita's thrusts. Uda pushed inside of her hard, anchoring Holly on her fake cock and biting down on the other side of her neck, holding Holly in place as she was fed on.

"Never disappoints," Nikita gasped, coming off Holly and taking out her fist from her pussy, and the gag from her mouth. Uda pulled herself from the girl as she pulled her cock from her, catching her as her legs buckled.

"Come here," Nikita said, disinfecting the bites on either side of Holly's neck and placing a plaster over both sets of bite marks. Holly moved absentmindedly to Nikita's instructions, Uda coming to sit next to her as she began to take the clothes around Holly's body off.

"Here," Uda said, reaching behind her and giving her an energy drink. Holly gave a weak smile, and half fell into Nikita's arms, closing her eyes, and she was embraced and gently rocked.

"I loved that, thank you, Mistresses," Holly softly said, receiving a kiss on both her cheeks from Uda and Nikita.

"The handcuffs were a nice touch," she said before yawning.

"Let's get you dried off and out of here,"

Uda said, standing up and being followed by Nikita, Holly still in her arms. Uda dried her body gently, applied a cream to her pussy and asshole, giving Nikita a playfully annoyed look as she saw the scratch marks, applying lotion to Holly's body before dressing her in a loose-fitting t-shirt and panties. Taking Holly from Nikita's arms, Uda carried Holly through the house and into her bedroom.

"Lay down for me," Uda softly said as she placed Holly down on her bed. Uda could hear the other girls playing cards in another room, one reading on her bed and two coming up behind her.

"Do you want us to look after her, Mistress?" Kelsey asked. Uda smiled. Kelsey was her favorite. Her feral cat personality yet, please love me, eyes melted Uda's cold heart every time.

"No, but you can get me a bottle of water and a protein bar," Uda replied, not bothering to turn around. She heard Kelsey walk off toward the small kitchen area where the girls kept their snacks, grabbing Hannah's wrist, who remained.

"Sit," Uda simply said to the girl, watching as Hannah sat on her lap and offered her wrist to Uda. Smiling, Uda shook her head.

"I just wanted you close," Uda replied, holding onto Hannah and feeling her relax into the embrace. Uda pulled a blanket over Holly, Kelsey leaving the snacks by her bedside. Uda stood up, hearing Nikita come into Holly's room, but stopping when Cleo came out of her room, her book still in her hand.

"Cleo," Nikita said, looking at her as Cleo began to blush. Nikita heard Cleo's heart pounding in her chest and smelt the ink in her veins. They had taken Cleo in three years ago. Their arrangement was simple. They wouldn't feed on a girl younger than 21 or older than 35. At 30, she was allowed to begin dating if she chose. After 35, Nikita and Uda would end the contract giving her one of two options. One, she could move out and find her way in the world while remaining in contact if she chose. Her life would be 100% hers. The second option was the same, with the addition of the bite. If a woman chose this option, Nikita and Uda would welcome her into their coven and teach her how to master and control her urges and powers. Most women chose the first option. After witnessing Nikita and Uda's lives for years, the novelty and excitement of the possibility to live forever soon worn off.

"Mistress," Cleo said, looking down, hoping that Nikita wouldn't notice the fresh tattoo on her body. Nikita had taken special care in training Cleo. Nikita liked the damaged ones, and it had taken her two years even to begin to gain Cleo's trust, her real trust. When Cleo had first been brought home, Nikita had known that she was only there because it was her best option. Cleo had been walking home after a late class in college, and some of the college boys on her campus had followed her. Nikita had been trying to waste the night away, bored, and looking for something to do while Uda was out of town dealing with trouble in another state. Nikita had smelt Cleo's vanilla scent mixed with fear, hearing the boys' quickening footsteps who were walking behind her. Deciding to play the hero, Nikita turned and began to follow them. They had walked for about a quarter-mile before one of them grabbed Cleo and threw her down on the ground. Nikita was surprised that it insulted her so much to hear the boys' heartbeats remained constant, as though stalking a girl and making her fearful did not mean anything to them in the slightest. She heard Cleo's hands trying to push one of the boys off her, scratching him and making Nikita smile.

"Good girl," Nikita said as she approached the group. Nikita had ripped the throats out of the two boys who tried to attack her, making her laugh, and watched as the other boy run away. That one was hit by a truck that was coming in the opposite direction, a happy coincidence.

"Well, that was unexpected," Nikita said as she watched the truck begin to slow down.

Cleo's face was a mix of relief and surprise, but it was her smile that made Nikita want her.

"You've got about 34 seconds to make a decision. You can come with me, knowing full well that I just murdered two boys by ripping their throats out. Don't worry. I'll explain everything later if you choose that one. Or, you can stay here and continue your life, explaining this to the authorities and hoping they believe you," Nikita said, just as the man jumped from his truck.

"I want to come with you. I don't know how to explain this," Cleo had replied, shrugging her shoulders.

"Wonderful," Nikita simply said, picking Nikita up and rushing her away from the scene.

"Cleo, take your shirt off," Nikita asked, Cleo, biting her bottom lip as following her instruction.

"See?" Nikita said to Uda, who looked at Cleo with suspicion.

"It's nothing," Cleo began to speak,

stopping when she saw the looks both Nikita and Uda were giving her.

"That is not nothing. That is a fucking tattoo," Uda replied, reaching out to grab Cleo's chin in her hand.

"What did I tell you when you asked if you could get one?" Uda said, Nikita, sitting down on the lounge as the other girls began to crowd around her slowly.

"What did I say, Cleo?" Uda repeated, slapping Cleo's left cheek.

"That I had to wait," Cleo replied, copping another slap across her face, this time on the right side.

"Let me help you. Wait for what?" Nikita called from the lounge. While Nikita and Uda may have been the most loving and caring Mistresses in their coven, they were still Mistresses nonetheless. And they ran their home like the well-designed BDSM dynamic, regardless of how accommodating they were to their girl's individual needs and desires.

"Wait until my next birthday," Cleo gasped as she felt Uda choke her.

"That's right. Which is only a month away," Uda said, throwing Cleo to the floor. Nikita watched as Cleo looked at her, raising an eyebrow.

"I'm not going to save you from something you got yourself into, darling," Nikita replied, causing Cleo to begin to cry.

"Yes, you'd better cry. Because the punishment I am going to give you will break your heart," Uda said, making Nikita roll her eyes.

She's always got to be so damn dramatic, Nikita thought to herself as she watched Uda go into Cleo's room and bring out her bed linen.

"Since you want to be as disobedient, like an ill-trained dog, you can sleep outside until I find a reason to want you back in my home," Uda said, causing the girls to look at Nikita, shocked.

"She knew what she was doing when she disobeyed us. She knew the consequences, just like you all do. Hell, you're the ones who come up with them, don't look so shocked when we action them," Nikita said, getting up and ripping the pillow out of Cleo's hands.

"Bitches don't need pillows," Nikita said before walking away and into her and Uda's bedroom, followed by Uda, leaving the girls speechless and Cleo whimpering.
Nikita was waiting for Uda at the edge of the bed.

"A little harsh!" Nikita exclaimed as Uda checked the time and began to undress.

"Said the one who took her pillow," Uda replied, beginning to take her clothes off.

"It's going to be a warm night. She'll be fine. It's not as though anything can hurt her out there," Uda added, kissing Nikita just for her to push her away.

"Oh, you want to play that game. You might be their Mistress, but I'm yours," Uda reminded Nikita, making her roll her eyes and begin to kiss Uda.

"That's better," Uda said through the kiss,

grabbing at Nikita and making her moan. Uda grabbed at Nikita's ass, throwing her down on the bed and ripping off her blouse.

"Yes," Nikita moaned as she felt Uda's hands on her breasts, grabbing at her passionately.

"What?!" Both Uda and Nikita aggressively yelled as they heard a knock coming from the opened bedroom door. As they turned to look toward the girl standing in the doorway, they instantly smelt her fear, only adding to their arousal.

Chapter 5

"Kelsey, come here," Nikita said, laying back on her elbows and waiting as Kelsey walked in. Uda eyed Nikita, who looked hungrily at Kelsey. They had girls on a nightly roster, making sure to supplement their thirst with blood taken from the local blood bank where Uda worked. That way, they made sure to keep their girls healthy, having one a night, and going to hunt once a week.

"I know that you ate earlier, but like, it's a Tuesday, so," Kelsey said, amusing Nikita with her indirect question. Kelsey had seen Nikita and Uda drinking from the blood bank bags that afternoon when she came home from the gym.

"So, you wanted to know if we still wanted you?" Nikita said, getting up and walking seductively over to where Kelsey had decided to stop. She had never been inside their bedroom in the five years she had been with them. Nodding, Kelsey felt Nikita's gaze unnerve her as she also felt Nikita's cold hand grab her wrist and throw her onto the bed and into Uda's arms.

"Why would we not want you, baby?" Uda moaned into Kelsey's ear, making her smile. Nikita slammed the door shut, smirking as the house shook from the impact, and joined Uda and Kelsey on the bed.

"What game should we play tonight, Kelsey?" Nikita said, licking the side of her top lip as she began to take off her clothes.

"Whatever you want, Mistress," Kelsey said, bending her head and avoiding Nikita's gaze. Uda began to undress Kelsey slowly, her touch sending shivers down Kelsey's spine, making her arch her back.

"Such a pretty little thing," Uda remarked, running her fingertips down Kelsey's back. While others in their coven ripped into the necks of their meals, Uda and Nikita enjoyed a more sexual approach and turned feeding time into playtime.

"Whatever I want?" Nikita questioned, making Uda roll her eyes. Uda loved how predatory Nikita got when she let herself lose some control and watched as Nikita wrapped her hand around Kelsey's neck and pulled her onto her stomach, making her gasp.

"I want you to fight me," Nikita demanded, taking Kelsey by surprise. Nikita pushed Kelsey's face down into the mattress until she kicked her legs and fought to break free, gasping and coming up for air as she was released.

"I mean, you won't win, but I appreciate the effort," Nikita said, sitting back raising an eyebrow, unimpressed. Kelsey looked hurt, so thinking twice before she decided to try something new, she slapped Nikita, taking her by surprise. Nikita deliberately ignored listening to her girls' thoughts when they played. It made for a far more heightened experience when she didn't know what would come next.

"Oh, yes," Nikita moaned. Although the impact did not hurt, she liked the rise in Kelsey's testosterone and grabbed the back of her head, kissing her deeply, softening as not to hurt Kelsey passed her limits. Uda came behind her, pulling her hips back and running her hands up her skirt, pulling her panties to the side and feeling her wetness.

"It's just me," Uda whispered as she took her strap on from her pants and began coating it in Kelsey's juices, making her jump and look behind her.

"Did I say you could turn around?" Nikita questioned aggressively, holding Kelsey's face in her hand as her other slapped her face. Kelsey felt Uda push into her making her moan as she was fish-hooked by Uda, who began to pound her rhythmically. Nikita kissed down Kelsey's breasts, biting into her as she was fucked from behind. Nikita pulled herself off Kelsey, leaving a bite mark in her the soft flesh of her breast and using her thumb to wipe the trickle of blood that escaped onto her own breasts. Uda could feel Kelsey become limp and lightheaded, smiling as she came on top of her before being pushed off Uda's lap.

"Come to me," Uda said, pulling Kelsey to her and feeding on Kelsey's other breast. They liked to feed on parts of their girls' bodies that were more difficult, as it meant they could suck deeper and harder without draining them. Coming up for air, Uda felt her eyes change, and their wicked glare matched with her smile turned Nikita on.

"How about you finish what you've started," Nikita said, laying down next to Kelsey as Uda climbed on top of her.

"I don't think you could take it," Uda teased, scratching Nikita's skin, making her smile. Kelsey gasped as a tear fell down her cheek, pausing Uda and Nikita in their tracks.

I just want to fuck you on top of her, Nikita said to Uda.

You can, but not right now, you know

that Uda replied, making Nikita roll her eyes and open her arms to Kelsey.

"Come here, baby," Nikita softening her expression and pulling Kelsey into her arms as she fought herself not to burst into tears.

"I'm okay, I promise, Mistress," Kelsey mumbled against Nikita's breast.

"Oh, shut up, you're a terrible liar," Nikita affectionately replied, pushing her nipple into Kelsey's mouth, genuinely smiling as she felt Kelsey begin to suckle. Uda placed a blanket over Kelsey and Nikita as Nikita began to rock Kelsey.

"You did so good, precious," Uda cooed, coming to sit next to Nikita and stroking Kelsey's cheek. Her furrowed forehead softened, and her eyes closed as she rolled into Nikita.

"My pretty girl," Nikita whispered as she bent her head and kissed Kelsey on the cheek.

***

"Hi girls," Nikita called as she walked into

the house. She wasn't expecting an answer. As much as she had enjoyed a couple of centuries or so of making her girls wait on her beckoned call, she had softened and allowed her recent pets to live their lives during the day, and night in almost complete freedom, depending on the roster.

"Hi Mistress," Eden softly said, unsure of the correct protocol and sitting up from the living room lounge. Nikita loved how untrained she was and smiled at her lovingly.

"Come and help me put this away. It is for you after all," Nikita said, watching as Eden put her phone and Air Pods down and walk over to her.

"Go and get them and bring them with you. I don't like your toys being left all over the house," Nikita instructed, placing her hands on her hips and enjoying the girl's scent of fear and arousal.

"Good girl," Nikita said, watching as Eden's wide-eyed gaze shifted to her once she had followed the instruction. Nikita tilted her head towards the bags of groceries on the bench and slapped Eden's ass playfully as she began to unpack the different foods and place them on the respective shelves. To make things easy, Uda had come up with a shelf system where everyone got their own, and a shopping list for everyone was placed on the fridge. Sure, they could go and get their groceries if they wished, but it was a nurturing task that Nikita enjoyed doing, much to her surprise.

"Holly said that you help them sometimes when they don't know what they want to be or do or whatever," Eden said, putting Hannah's almond milk in the fridge.

"Mmm," Nikita replied, pouring herself a drink.

"Go on," she added, seeing Eden waiting for her permission.

"I was wondering if you could help me too. I don't know what I want to do, but maybe something with yoga could be cool. Like, I'd love to learn it and maybe do some online stuff like Hannah does with her artworks, maybe even end up with a studio of my own," Eden said, making Nikita smile as her eyes lit up with delight over the possibilities.

"Fabulous. I can imagine you having a successful studio. I'll discuss it with Uda," Nikita replied, running her hands over Eden's neck, breathing her in and holding her close before kissing the top of her head and walking away.

"Thank you," Eden said, smiling at the ground.

"Thank you, Mistress," Nikita corrected, as she walked toward Eden, intimidatingly so.

"Thank you, Mistress," Eden replied, kissing Nikita back as she pressed her lips to hers.

"What did she say?" Hannah asked when Eden walked out to the pool. It was a sunny Saturday afternoon, and the girls were lounging around the pool. This was the first sun they had seen in months as the harsh winter had slowly begun to break.

"She said she'd ask Uda about it," Eden replied, Hannah, giving her an encouraging look.

"They discuss everything together. But it's a pretty simple request. I doubt they'll say no," Hannah said before diving into the pool. Eden sat at the edge of the pool and observed her surroundings. The backyard was immaculately kept, thanks to several gardeners that came during the week. The large trees which overhung the fire pit made the area look like something from a country living magazine, and the two hot tubs on either side of the pool evened the space out. She looked into the gym area where Kelsey and Cleo were working out with the personal trainer who came daily to the house. Eden gazed up to the top porch, looking into Uda's and Nikita's bedroom window, seeing Holly's hands pressed against the window as Uda wrapped her arm around her neck and locked her eyes onto Eden as she slowly bit into Holly's neck, holding her firmly as her legs buckled and gave way. She was watching as Nikita joined her, stroking Holly's cheeks and biting down on the other side of her neck. Water splashed on Eden's face, breaking her trance-like gaze and causing her to look at Nerada with playful confusion.

Nerada had been spotted by Uda when she went to the blood bank to donate blood at Uda's previous blood bank location. Every 15 years, she needed to move to a different location. She could only share her skincare routine so many times when she looked 35 but was meant to be 50. Uda had taken more blood from Nerada, interested to see her, drainability, as Nikita liked to put it. After 4L, even Uda was impressed that Nerada was still conscious and stopped, but knew that she wanted her. So she had monitored her over the following days, curious to see how she functioned on so little. Nerada had hopped on the subway, ready to go to work but had missed her stop as she had passed out and into Uda's arms.

"Are you coming in?" Nerada asked. Eden gazed at her toned stomach, flawless and youthful face and skin, and had to admit, the lifestyle Uda and Nikita gave in exchange for a little blood was second to none. Eden giggled and jumped in, feeling the cool and refreshing water wash away any fear or doubts she had that she had made the right discussion.

Chapter 6

"Is Cleo coming, Mistress?" Kelsey asked as the girls began to get ready. It had become a tradition that the household spent Saturday nights together, and this week it had been decided that they would play paintball and get burgers afterward for dinner. As per the contract, Nerada was able to date and begin to form a human lifestyle away from Uda and Nikita and had a date that evening.

"With Nerada out for the evening, our numbers will be uneven if she comes," Uda replied, going to the window and looking down on Cleo. The sun might have been out all day, but the nights were still cold, with the leftover frost from winter managing to creep in almost every night. Cleo had been outside for the last three days, but Nikita and Uda could still smell the acid from the ink running through her veins.

"Another night won't kill her," Nikita added, turning to face Kelsey, giving her the only answer she'd be getting. Accepting that it wasn't something to press on, Kelsey nodded her head, sat on the lounge, and tied up her sneakers.

We're bringing her in tomorrow, right? Nikita asked Uda, the worry in her thoughts making her laugh.

I was going to bring her in after we got back, Uda replied, sensing Nikita's relief.

"Let's go," Uda called, satisfied with the despair Cleo felt as she turned the lights off and made her way to the front door.

She's crying, Uda, Nikita thought as they got in their Maserati and began to drive off. The girls were following in Holly's jacked up truck, a gift from Uda and Nikita after her first bite. They had thought that she would want something more feminine, but a huge, don't fuck with me, black luxury truck with all the fittings was all her heart desired.

Good, Uda simply replied, making Nikita

scoff. She hated how Uda always pressed on the girls' limits.

"She's not a puppy, Nikita. She's not your baby. I hated having to have a frozen meal. Holly was just a bonus. Don't forget what they are, despite how deeply you feel toward them, despite the life we give them," Uda said out loud, enraging Nikita.

"You sound just like them," Nikita replied, referring to the others in their coven who opposed the gentle and loving ways they treated their pets. Nikita was further enraged as she held onto Cleo's mind for as long as she could before Uda drove her out of reach.

Stopping at the paintball field, Nikita got out of the car and began to walk away from Uda, just for Uda to run to catch up to her and grab her by the upper arm and spin her around. Holly, Kelsey, Eden, and Hannah looked on, guessing that it was about Cleo.

You're such a fucking bitch to Cleo, Nikita said, tired of holding back.

The disrespect that she showed us was out of line, yes. But she doesn't view us as only their Mistresses. It goes deeper than that, and know that! Nikita exclaimed, the pleading in her voice making Uda disappointed. Uda had burned whole towns to the ground after one person had dared to insult Nikita, and it pained her that firstly, she could no longer do that, and secondly, that it was her that now hurt Nikita so profoundly.

I don't care that they all call them pets and treat theirs with such contempt. Give them limiting lives if they get lives at all. Regardless of how disobedient they are, I love my girls, they are my babies, Uda, and this punishment has gone on for too long, Nikita added, the final blow and last

You are getting soft in your old age. I'm sorry. I'll bring her inside the moment we get home, Uda replied, embracing Nikita and kissing her passionately before walking over to join the girls.

"We aren't fighting anymore," Uda said to Hannah, wrapping her arm around her as they walked. Uda had to admit, Nikita was right. These girls did fill the void in her heart to be needed and loved for all that she was. It made her time on earth less lonely. Hannah beamed up at Uda, making her roll her eyes as they began to get fitted out for their competition.

"Teams?" The man who ran the park asked.

"I think it needs to everyone for herself tonight," Nikita quickly said, making the girls laugh.

They were given their instructions, taught how to shoot and reload as a group of men walked in behind them. The girls seemed oblivious, but Uda and Nikita knew the scent by heart.

Hunters, Nikita fearfully said to Uda, who looked at her out of the corner of her eye.

They won't start something here. They might not even know who we are, Uda replied, standing up and looking at the group of men who looked at them menacingly.

"Ready, sis?" Kelsey asked Uda, having seen the fearful look Nikita had given Uda. Uda looked at Kelsey amused, enjoying how observant the girl was before clearing her throat.

"Yeah, let's go," Uda replied. Usually, her voice was smooth and smoldering, the type you'd expect from a seductress, but that wasn't something she was trying to be right now as her fake voice echoed through Kelsey's ears. She felt Uda's hand on the back of her neck as she was walked to the field, Holly stopping once they were all huddled behind an old barn shed.

"Hunters?" Kelsey asked Nikita, rolling her eyes dramatically. She looked at Eden, knowing that they were going to have to explain.

"So, there are some armies in the world, and all they do is try to find and then kill our kind. Those men in there are all members of that army. They are who we call the Hunters," Uda explained to Eden. Eden had noticed the tattoo on one of the man's arm. It was the same tattoo her Father had before he had gone insane after her Mother had died. He had taken a sharp knife and cut it out of his body, burning it and then drinking his weight in alcohol night and day from then on. Eden didn't think now was the time to rehash old family stories and bit her bottom lip. It was unnerving, to say the least, to see Uda and Nikita afraid.

"So, no paintball?" Hannah asked, making Kelsey laugh, and Nikita tilt her head.

"Great observation," Uda sarcastically replied, reaching her hand out to Hannah and stroking her cheek affectionately.

"We need to get home, to get out of here. Do you all still have your bags in the trunks of your cars?" Uda asked, seeing the girls nod their heads.

"Eden, yours is in our car. You'll come with us," Nikita said, taking her hand and running toward the outer laying fence. The girls followed, hearing the men begin to walk out of the training shed.

"Hurry up," Uda hissed at them, annoyed that human legs were so slow. Nikita ripped a hole in the fence as the men began shouting at each other. Filing the girls through, Uda ran to the truck and started it before starting her car and throwing her paint gun in the back seat.

"Seatbelt," Nikita said to Eden whose heart was pounding so loudly that Uda decided to sit in the back with her.

"Come here," Uda said, reaching out to hold a shaking Eden as Nikita flooded it, followed by Holly, speeding away and making the men look up from their game.

"Is this, like, a normal sort of thing that happens?" Eden asked as Uda stroked her hair.

"No," Uda simply replied.

They knew Demelza. That was a show of force. To show that they can reach us, Uda said to Nikita, who adjusted her rear vision mirror.

I know, Nikita replied, wanting to get back to Cleo.

"Right, Nerada," Nikita said to Uda, who

was already taking out her phone.

"Nothing," Uda said, hanging up the phone as she heard it go to voice mail.

"Fuck," Nikita yelled, slamming the steering wheel and making Eden jump.

"It's alright, we aren't going to let anything bad happen to you," Uda whispered in Eden's ear, her seductive tone sending chills down Eden's body.

They pulled up to the house as Cleo ran from the yard, covered in blood.

"The fuck?" Nikita questioned, jumping out of the car and running to Cleo.

"I'm sorry, I am so sorry," Cleo begged. Nikita's eyes turned as her hands were drenched in the blood coming from Cleo's stomach. Holly pulled up behind them, Uda slamming the door shut as she tried to get out.

"Stay in the car," she commanded in a tone that froze Holly in her place. Uda slowly paced back and forth, thinking quickly. This was an attack.

"What are you sorry for?" Nikita asked, picking Cleo up and carrying her inside.

"They came, and they wouldn't stop until I told them where you were," Cleo cried. Nikita stopped in her tracks. She hadn't smelt Cleo's blood on the Hunters. She hadn't picked up her scent.

"They've got new toys," Uda said, beckoning to Holly that she was allowed to leave the truck, as the four girls ran to catch up to Nikita and Uda.

Placing Cleo on the kitchen bench, Uda turned the lights on and inspected the house.

"They didn't try to hide their stench in here," she said with dismay. Holly had obediently stolen medical equipment at the request of her Mistresses for years, turning the kitchen bench into what resembled an ER room.

"Girls, go downstairs and pack, Hannah, pack for Cleo and Kelsey, help Eden. We won't be coming back here. It's not home anymore," Uda instructed before turning back to Cleo.

"Yes, Mistress," Hannah and Kelsey said in unison, taking Eden's hand and racing down the corridor toward the basement.

Nikita was helping Holly to try and stop the bleeding, Uda looking into Cleo's fading eyes.

"Holly," Uda calmly said, as Holly frantically looked up.

"I can do it, Mistress, I can," Holly began to cry as Uda looked at Nikita.

She betrayed us, Demi, Uda thought, Nikita, tilting her head in anger before looking back down at Cleo.

"No, you can't, Holly," Nikita softly said, taking her hands away and holding onto Holly as she cried in Nikita's arms.

"Go and pack," Uda simply instructed, Holly's eyes angry and challenging as Uda stepped forward.

"I said go," Uda repeated equally as calmly, as Holly reminded herself who she was challenging and bent her head in submission.

"Yes, Mistress," Holly sighed, walking away and leaving Uda and Nikita alone with Cleo.

She will not forgive us easily, Nikita said, reading Holly's angry mind as she slammed the door to the basement.

She should remember what we are and that our humanity is a choice, not an instinct or obligation, Uda said, running her hands over Cleo's bloodied body and sucking her blood-covered fingertip.

She betrayed us and put us all in danger, Uda thought, catching Nikita's eye.

What should she have done, Uda? Died for us? Nikita replied, raising an eyebrow.

Yes. She will, anyway. We can't take her with us. She's too weak and will slow us down, Uda answered, making Nikita roll her eyes.

What will tell the girls? That we had to take her to the farm so she could run free with the other pups? Nikita said, looking down at Cleo as she gasped for air.

"It won't hurt, baby," Nikita softly said, holding Cleo close as she bit down as gently as she could muster as she began to feed.

"I'm sorry," Cleo gasped, breaking Uda's heart more than she cared to admit.

"You don't need to be sorry. You've done nothing wrong," Uda replied, biting into her and draining the last of her blood, feeling Cleo become peaceful.

"They're ready," Holly said, coming behind Nikita and Uda and looking down at Cleo before looking up at them, her eyes angry and tear-filled.

"I understand, Mistresses," Holly softly said, placing a sheet over Cleo's body.

"Get them in their cars. Holly, there can be no weak links now. The Hunters have declared war, by coming here, by coming to find us simply to show their presence," Uda explained. She smelt Holly shift in mood, and she raised an eyebrow.

"She did it to herself. Everyone knows

what they are signing. But, Mistress, if it comes to me, make it hurt," Holly replied, making Nikita laugh.

"My pleasure, my little masochist," she said, choking Holly and kissing her before throwing her backward.

"Now obey your Mistress," Nikita yelled, walking to their bedroom, followed by Uda.

"That was more dramatic than you needed to be," Uda said, packing her bags in a hurry.

"Oh, baby, you've seen nothing yet," Nikita replied, looking hungrily at Uda. Cleo's blood pulse through her and made her head spin in a frenzy as she too packed.

While they both had several bags of possessions in several locations, after being in this house for 12 years, they had collected extensive collections of clothes, shoes, and jewelry, not to mention technical gadgets and weaponry.

"Ready?" Uda asked, waiting for her at the door as she heard the cars rev their engines outside. It had been over a decade since Uda and

Nikita found their last battle, taking out the wife of the Hunter who had tormented them for years, finally ending his quest as he saw them feed and fuck the love of his life. It had been no trouble at all to seduce her, and the sweetness of her blood had tasted like vanilla liquor as they bathed in it. They left her body in front of him. They had chained him to the wall of their last dungeon, knowing that he would be found and rescued once the house was alight.

"Ready," Nikita replied, kicking over the last bucket of gasoline as she carried a bottle in her hand through the house, lighting it of fire and watching as flames raced through the house.

Eden sat in the back of the car, amongst the leather travel bags, and turned around to see the house she had grown to call home go up in flames. This is how she assumed the house had looked, which her father had been saved from when she was 11 years old. She knew that now was not the time to ask where they were going, what would happen next, or if they could stop to get food. She hadn't eaten since lunch, and her stomach rumbled from the back seat.

"We will get something to eat soon, sweetie," Uda said from the front without turning around.

"It's okay, I'm not that hungry," Eden replied, not wanting to be the reason for slowing down the plan her Mistresses had.

"We don't think you're tough pushing through your limits or lying to us," Nikita said, looking in the rear vision mirror.

"No matter how noble your intentions are," she added, reading Eden's mind and smiling.

"I never seem to get anything right," Eden muttered, looking out the window.

"You're not meant to right now. You're still being trained," Uda replied, seeing Eden's fear.

"Don't worry, it's not difficult to obey the rules," she added, satisfied when Eden gave a weak smile and turned to look back out the window.

Nikita and Uda were driving to an esteemed member of the Order. Heidi Sullivan. She had been turned the same year as Nikita. The three of them had been in the Order at the same time, completing many successful missions together. Heidi accepted Nikita and Uda's lifestyle with their girls out of respect for Nikita and Uda's power and status within the coven. However, she never kept women like they did. She preferred the hunt.

Heidi lived three hours away in a small town to hide in but big enough that no one cared when people went missing. It was the perfect hunting ground. There was always some deserving snack with impure thoughts and tendencies who needed killing, and Heidi took it upon herself to rid the city of them.

As Uda drove up Heidi's long driveway, she smelt Heidi's last meal and had to control herself.

"You're not the only one who is hungry," she said more to herself than to Eden. The house was less luxurious than the home Eden had become accustomed to. The ranch-style home was in stark contrast to the sports cars and luxury truck, which pulled up outside. Heidi appeared in her home doorway, crossing her arms across her chest and waiting as she saw Uda and Nikita exit the car.

"Stay," Nikita said to Eden, who buckled her seatbelt back up.

"My my, things must have well and truly hit the fan if I'm the person you have turned to," Heidi laughed as she embraced Uda and Nikita.

"You don't even want to know," Uda replied. Heidi smirked.

"Oh, but I do. You can put your pets out the back. I'll get my men to feed them and give them water," Heidi remarked, enjoying the agitation in Nikita's face.

"Thank you for your hospitality," Nikita forced out, knowing full well that if Heidi were to turn them away, they would lose the protection of the coven, something that they desperately needed if they were to get out of this alive. Uda walked up the steps, clicked her fingers at the girls, and watched as they took their bags from their cars and made their way to her.

"Go with, whoever the fuck you are. I hope you like camping," Uda said, referring to the semi-naked man standing next to her. The girls looked at each other and then back to Uda.

"Did I stutter?" Uda asked, annoyed that she was questioned, watching as the girls followed the man toward the backyard.

"Last time one of us was outside," Nerada muttered. She was still bitter about her date being cut short, coping a slap across the face from Uda.

"Don't you dare," Uda threatened, happy that Nerada looked her challenging eyes to the ground as her cheek turned bright red. Uda was always reminded how much freedom she gave her girls when she saw the way others treated their pets, and it made her frustrated that they dared to defy her when they could be living a far less fulfilling lifestyle.

Uda and Nikita spent the next few hours talking with Heidi, catching up, and feasting on her hospitality.

"I've said it, and I'll repeat it. I do not know how you can control yourselves. You collect the most divine morsels, then torture yourselves for years only sampling from them," Heidi said as she let the boy in her lap drop to the floor, just as Hannah appeared in the doorway.

"One of your pups seems lost," Heidi teased, wiping the corner of her mouth. Hannah's stomach rumbled, and she looked at Nikita and Uda in distress.

"What is it, honey?" Nikita asked, extending her hand to Hannah.

"There isn't enough to eat for all of us," Hannah whispered, taking Nikita's hand and stepping over the bodies on the carpeted floor before sitting next to Nikita, who stroked her hair and held her close.

"Maybe you should have fought harder for your share then?" Heidi asked.

"I feed my pets once a day. It's all about natural selection. If they aren't strong enough, then they don't eat. That's why they are in such peak shape," Heidi remarked, running her nails over the tight, chiseled abs of the man standing next to her in nothing but latex pants and a collar around his neck.

"I know you do things a little differently in your house, but you aren't in your house anymore, are you pet?" Heidi said, standing up and sitting next to Hannah before she could register what was happening.

"Oh, don't be scared. It spoils the taste," Heidi said, pulling Hannah's wrist toward her mouth before biting down into her and making her wail. Nikita and Uda's touch was like silk compared to the burning sensation that racked

Hannah's body as Heidi aggressively ripped into her. Coming up for air, Heidi laughed as she flung Hannah back into the arms of Nikita, who hushed her by covering her mouth with her hand and tried to soothe her by whispering in her ear lovingly.

"That's how a real Vampire feels," Heidi hissed as tears streamed down Hannah's face.

"You've had your fun. If you touch any of my girls again, I will burn you alive, Heidi," Nikita calmly said, coping a look of combative fury from Heidi. Uda simply placed the woman she was feasting on the floor and hissed at Heidi with an ancient power that silenced Heidi and made her raise her eyebrow.

"Consider it noted," Heidi replied. Although she held the seat to The Order, she knew that Uda, even in her dieting state, was stronger and more powerful than she was, and she was sure to lose in combat with Nikita also by Uda's side.

"Feed the girls until they are satisfied,"

she said to her man. Nikita, leaving with Hannah to make sure it was done and wanting to check on her girls.

"Mistress," Eden squealed as Nikita walked down the stairs and into the small guest house that the girls had set themselves up in. The other's turned around, smiling as they saw Nikita stand in the doorway.

"Hello, baby," Nikita replied, coming to sit down next to Eden, who flung her arms around her making her laugh.

"Were you worried, little one?" Nikita asked Eden, who gave her big puppy dog eyes and nodded her head.

"We all were when we heard the screams," Nerada said, seeing Hannah's bruised arm and looking up at Nikita.

"Heidi. She does things her way," Nikita replied to Nerada's gaze.

You could have stopped her, Nerada bitterly thought, Nikita, looking at her in disdain but deciding not to address it, as she let Eden go.

"How long are we going to be here, Mistress?" Kelsey asked, coming to sit next to Nikita and placing her head on her lap. Nikita stroked Kelsey's hair, looking around at their surroundings.

"Hopefully, only a week. We need to deal with the Hunters. We don't know if they know where our other homes are. So, funnily enough, this happens to be the safest place for us right now," Nikita explained as she heard Uda come down the stairs.

"And, on that note. Nerada, come," Uda said, coming in just to say that before walking back out, Nerada following her fearfully.

"It's not about that," Nikita said, grabbing her wrist and referring to Nerada's thought she had minutes earlier, instantly putting her at ease and an apologetic look coming over her face. Nerada walked to where Uda was standing, and her stomach tightened as she saw Uda hold her contract in her hands.

"I don't know how long this is going to take. I don't want the rest of your life put on hold and made difficult. I know you want children. We should consider ending this tonight, making you free to go but free to stay if you choose. I want you to have the life you've been trying to build for yourself. You won't be able to continue if we hold you to this," Uda explained as Nikita walked to where they stood.

"I don't know what life is meant to be like without you," Nerada tearfully said.

"And you don't need to explore that right now. This isn't a rejection. This is freedom. Freedom to stay, but the freedom to leave whenever you desire, three years early because we cannot promise you that it will be done and sorted in that time," Nikita explained, wiping Nerada's tears away.

"You'll always be safe in my arms," Nikita added, pulling Nerada in close and holding her affectionately until Nerada relaxed into the embrace.

"I want children, yes, but I could always just get knocked up by some guy in a pub. I don't necessarily need the white picket fence and perfect husband," Nerada replied, making Uda laugh.

"Then have that. But we want to do this for you," she said, Nerada nodding her head as Uda kissed her and torn up the contract, handing it to Nerada.

"You'll always be my baby," Uda said, as Nerada sighed.

"I want to stay though, I mean, right now, where would I even go?" Nerada laughed.

"You have a point. Don't tell the others. This isn't for them," Nikita said as she kissed Nerada, biting her lip and winking at her.

"Don't you have to ask permission or something for that now," Nerada laughed.

"Try and tell me you don't like it," Uda whispered, her appetite forming a different type of hunger.

"I couldn't lie to you," Nerada moaned,

nodding her head as she felt Nikita's hands come from behind her and over her body.

"Good girl," Uda smiled, grabbing Nerada's wrist in her hand and walking her back to the house.

"Where are they?" Eden asked, popping her head out the door 2 hours later, making Holly, Hannah, and Kelsey laugh.

"Probably fucking," Kelsey replied, painting her toenails. Eden took a breath.

"But Nerada has a boyfriend," she said, making Holly smirk.

"You've seen Nikita and Uda, haven't you? Like you haven't missed the fact that one seductive glace from them stops your entire world from turning. Even the straightest woman has no defense against their power," Hannah said, surprised that Eden was surprised.

"Anyway, sex is sex. If it feels good, why limit yourself?" Holly questioned just as Nerada stumbled back into the room.

"Well, speak of the devil," Holly said, watching as Nerada collapsed on the bed.

"You called," Uda said, startling Holly and making Kelsey mess up her nail polish, making them all smirk.

"Good night, babies," Uda said, leaving them for the evening and going back to Nikita, who she had waiting for her in bed.

Chapter 7

"That went according to plan. For creatures who have been alive for so long, they are quite unoriginal in their retreat methods," a man said, walking into the circled room where Zagan waited patiently.

"How did it go? Nerada missed three phone calls but answered the fourth. She had to leave in a hurry. So it worked?" Zagan asked more eagerly than he wanted to. He hated not being a part of the fight, rather, the distraction.

"It went perfectly. Your Intel was right. They were at the paintball fields. They saw us and left before fighting a single ball. I assume they went back to their main house, found the present we left for them," another man sneered, laughing with a third man who walked inside.

"What present?" Zagan asked. He had not been aware that anything would occur more than the men showing themselves to Uda and Nikita.

"Well. One of the girls had stayed behind and was outside in the hot tub, so we have a little bit of fun with her before heading to the paintball field. She is surely dead by now, a message that no one is safe. If you consort with Vampires, you are as much as a Vampire as a real one," a final man said. The four leaders of the four Hunter families sat in a circle, Zagan sitting on the lounge outside of the circle.

We never agreed on hurting humans, Zagan thought, surprised that the men had done the things they had done.

"So, what now?" Zagan asked, brushing the thought to the side and lean forward.

"Now, we wait. We have bugged the cars which remained on the property with trackers. It won't be long before we can find them again. The Hunt has begun," the man with the brass handle on his walking stick said before entering the room, the four leaders standing almost immediately, Zagan following suit.

"Sit. We have much to discuss," the man said, gesturing to the men to follow him as he opened a secret door and walking through the entryway.

***

"You wanted to talk to me?" Heidi questioned, walking out into the garden where Uda was standing. The full moon illuminated the night, and as Uda stood looking up at the stars, she wondered what it would feel like to die.

"Yes. Let's cut to the chase. What will it take to get you to help us kill these Hunters?" Uda replied, not wanting to waste a moment. She knew that the Hunters would be tracking them. She knew their days were numbered if they didn't put up some defenses. Heidi looked at Uda, then looked toward where the girls were sleeping.

"Hannah. I want Hannah," Heidi simply answered, somewhat taking Uda by surprise.

"We don't keep slaves anymore Heidi, I can't give you someone like that," Uda replied, annoyed that it was going to take some serious bargaining to sway Heidi. She was still living in a time where humans held no worth, merely there to be feasted upon and used as entertainment.

"Come on. Surely you can turn a blind eye to one human. There are plenty of others that you could choose from," Heidi teased. Uda tried to connect to Nikita, but she was too far away.

"I need to," Uda began to say, being silenced by Heidi.

"You need to speak to Nikita, I know. But my advice, don't take too long. I have more important things to worry about than some Hunters chasing two of the best warriors I have ever had. I am honestly surprised that you two are so fearful of them. Sure, their weapons have had an upgrade, but with all your experience and skill, why are you so shaken?" Heidi asked, turning back toward the house and walking away before Uda could reply.

"Because now they kill humans for sport as well," Uda muttered to herself, annoyed more than anything that Heidi had not named a price she was more willing to pay.

"Put your pets to bed?" Uda said as she saw Nikita come back into the main house, making Nikita smirk.

"Yes," she playfully replied, coming to sit down next to Uda and wrapping her body up in hers.

"Have you heard anything from Heidi?" Nikita asked, wishing that they had been given the news about whether she was going to help them or not. Uda didn't want to tell Nikita the terms of Heidi's help and sighed heavily.

"She wants one of our girls," Uda said, unable to look Nikita in the eye.

"Is she out of her fucking mind?!" Nikita yelled, Uda, rolling her eyes.

"You're going to wake them all up," she plainly said, getting up and bringing Nikita a bottle of whiskey.

"She is so bloody sadistic. I don't want her having any of them. They all have such specific needs and requirements. Heidi can't think that she could effectively meet them?" Nikita said. It annoyed her that Heidi dared to request such a price for her help.

"She wants Hannah," Uda said, deciding that holding off telling Nikita wouldn't help. Nikita threw the bottle into the fire, making it rage as she turned to face Uda, the flames lighting the burning fury in her eyes.

"Never," Nikita said with an intensity Uda had no predicted. Nikita snarled aggressively at the notion, Uda bowing her head.

"I told her we would think about it. She has given us three hours. We have two to go," Uda said, as Nikita placed her hand on her neck and pushed her against the wall, making the house shake.

"How dare you!" Nikita growled from deep within her being. Uda snarled back, pushing Nikita's arm away.

"What would you have us do?!" Uda growled back, the fire in her eyes igniting in response to Nikita's fury. Over the last 950 years, there had only been a handful of times that Uda had seen Nikita so enraged, and it made her agitated that this time was over a human.

"Have you forgotten how easy you let Cleo go?! This is the same thing," Uda said, walking to the bar and taking the first bottle she could reach, beginning to drink.

"No, it's not," Nikita said, settling into the sadness of the decision.

"She will kill her. Give her Kelsey. She's a freak. She would enjoy the pain Heidi will put her through. Hannah can't take it. It will destroy her," Nikita said, looking up at Uda, her eyes full of sadness and misery. Uda just took another mouthful of liquor before putting the bottle down.

"She didn't ask for Kelsey," Uda remarked, annoyed that she was being challenged.

"And if she had?!" Nikita yelled, not caring who she woke up anymore, "I will not let you do this." Uda's eyes went wide as she processed the words that Nikita was saying to her.

"Do not stand in my way. This isn't about one girl. It's about all of us!" Uda shouted, slamming her fist down on the kitchen bench.

"There is no, all of us if we keep losing them! We lost Cleo. I am not losing anyone else, Uda!" Nikita shouted back, hearing the girls making their way inside, wondering what was going on.

"We will discuss this later," Uda snarled.

"There is nothing to discuss. If you come for Hannah, I will never forgive you," Nikita said, just as the girls walked into the living room.

"What's going on?" Nerada asked, speaking for the other women.

"Would you believe us if we said nothing?" Uda replied, still looking at Nikita dead in the eye.

"No, absolutely not," Kelsey said, coming to sit on the lounge, her expectant eyes melting Uda's heart.

"Fine, we won't get Heidi's help," she said to Nikita, finally understanding why Nikita wouldn't want to give Heidi up as she looked into Kelsey's eyes. Nikita sat down on the lounge, pulled Hannah into her arms, and held her as the others sat down, waiting for an explanation as to why they were woken up by their Mistresses aggressive shouting.

"If we want to get Heidi's help. As in, the help from The Order to get the Hunters away from us," Uda began to explain.

"She wanted Hannah," Nikita finished, looking down at Hannah, the fear in her eyes making Nikita shake her head.

"We aren't giving you to her, baby, don't worry, Mommy wasn't going to let that happen," Nikita said, kissing the top of Hannah's head and pushing her face into her cleavage, holding her there with her hand as her face burned red.

"So, we're on our own?" Holly asked, biting her bottom lip. Uda and Nikita looked at each other and shrugged their shoulders.

"Yeah," they said in unison.

"The Order isn't going to help us directly. They'll still hunt these bastards, but they won't be specifically hunting the ones we will be fighting," Uda explained, Eden nodding her head.

"Get your dogs and guns, girls. We're going hunting," she said, making everyone laugh.

"We have a friend in the Russian mountains, Ursula. We'll go there. Unfortunately, Holly, Nerada, you'll need to come with us, meaning your jobs. You have none now. That boy you were seeing, you have to leave him behind," Uda added, Nerada nodding her head slowly, trying to hide her disappointment. She hadn't been able to give Zagan a reason why she had to up and go, so suddenly, the night of the paintball game, she was happy that he hadn't seemed too bothered. Since then, he had sent her a few texts, but she had ignored all of them, deciding that it was better to ghost him than try to drag him into this life.

Holly twisted her mouth bitterly.

"Don't worry about your practice. It'll still go ahead. We just need to take a moment to figure out how many we need to kill and what part of our old life is safe to continue with. Have we ever let you down?" Nikita asked, opening her arm to Holly, who came to snuggle into her.

"No," Holly softly replied, Nikita, kissing her cheek.

"Get your stuff together. I guess tonight is as good as ever to leave," Uda said, making sure the girls' watches were synced before letting them leave to pack.

"I feel like I only just unpacked," Eden moaned as she walked back to her room.

"Get used to it, maybe go for an online business model right now, because I don't see this ending and going back to normal anytime soon," Nerada said to Eden, who looked overwhelmed at the thought of going on the run.

Chapter 8

Ursula had lived in the mountains all her life, as was her family's way. She knew the forest. Its trees and ridges, gullies, and rises ran through her veins from a hundred years of DNA mapping. She lived in her family's ancestral land, in the home her grandfather had built over 100 years ago with his Father and Grandfather. Ursula had renovated parts of the large house over the years, but the huge farmhouse with its six bedrooms, three bathrooms, high ceilings, and large fireplace in the middle of the living room had all remained.

"Jax, let's go," Ursula plainly said as she summoned her Russian bear dog. Jax stretched her long legs, shook her heavy fur coat, and walked toward Ursula and out the door. The snow had been falling hard that night, covering any unprotected surface in snow a foot deep. The snow was still lightly falling, but Ursula had kept Jax in the house for long enough and knew that she needed to run before she became too painfully hyperactive.

They walked out toward the forest, a raven flying overhead and making Ursula question the intention for the day. Although not a particularly spiritual woman, Ursula could not deny the universe and its patterns.

"Something is going to change for us today, Jax," she muttered to herself, seeing Jax's tail disappear behind a tree before she began barking.

"Sooner rather than later," Ursula said, again to herself as she ran to see what had caught Jax's attention. Ursula had never been described as slender or athletic, yet her strong, mountain woman build gave her an advantage when running through the snow. She reached Jax in a matter of seconds, freezing when she saw what had taken her curiosity. A young woman of around 23 lean and freezing, chained to a tree wearing only a pair of boots. Ursula, who always carried an axe with her when she went walking through the woods, pulled it from her belt and broke the frozen chains, catching the girl as her legs gave way. Ursula was not even sure if the woman was still alive, her limp body blue from hypothermia, and the apparent beating she had been subjected to.

"Jax, scout," Ursula instructed, the dog running off through the trees to inspect the area and make sure that it was safe. The last thing Ursula wanted was any trouble as she rescued the girl. Taking her heavy coat off, Ursula wrapped it around the woman and held her close as she saw Jax re-emerge, beginning to take the girl home.

Ursula kicked the door open, Jax running inside and making quick work of patrolling the property before barking once and settling by the fire. Ursula carried the younger woman inside, her black hair wet from the snow as she placed her exhausted body down by the fire, Jax, moving out of the way. Ursula went to the kitchen, pouring a large amount of water into a pot, and turned on the stove. She placed a spoonful of camomile tea into the water and drizzled in some honey, turning the heat up before walking back to find the girl breathing slightly more deeply. Ursula sat next to the girl, the morning sun rising behind the trees' tips as the fire warmed the living room. She should be heading into town to her store by now. Ursula owned a coat and hat store, the only one who still used traditional tailoring in the town. However, she knew that she was not about to leave the fragile girl alone.

"Silvia, you will need to open the store for me today. I won't be in. Possibly for the rest of the week as well," Ursula said, leaving a voice message for the woman who was second in charge.

"There, now that everything is taken care of, let's put this little girl back together," Ursula said, talking to Jax. She got up from her kneeling position next to the girl as she heard the pot on the stove beginning to boil. Taking the pot, she drained the tea, removing any floating camomile, and poured the liquid into a mug, bringing it back to the girl. Ursula placed the tea down, gently lift the girl into her strong arms, and held her against her voluptuous breasts before taking the mug and warming the girl's lips with the tea. She knew that the girl would be too weak to drink but was delighted when she saw her tongue lick her lips.

"That's it, good girl," Ursula said, seeing the girl's eyes flutter open as she felt the liquid touch her lips once more. Ursula looked into the woman's eyes, their piercing green taking Ursula by surprise. It was uncommon for eyes such as these to be found in the mountain area. Most people had either blue or brown. Ursula's own blue eyes twinkled as she saw the woman's eye glaze over, still too weak and too cold to focus.

"You're alright," Ursula gently said,

allowing the girl one final sip before placing her back down gently and leaving her by the fire for a moment. The fire had begun to dry her hair, but Ursula knew that she needed to find warm clothes for the girl to wear. As comfortable and warm as Ursula's coat was, she knew that the woman would be frightened when she woke up, and being clothed would make the whole situation slightly less frightening.

Ursula went to her bedroom, opened the door to her wardrobe, and took out a pair of socks, warm sweat pants, and a t-shirt. She knew that the house would be warm enough and that the blankets she was planning on tucking around the girl would suffice. Coming back to the living room, Ursula carefully took off the boots, frowning when she saw the woman was not wearing any socks. The boots had stuck to her skin, causing the woman to wince in her semi-unconscious state as the pain of removing the leather ran through her body.

"I'm sorry, darling, I know it hurts,"

Ursula affectionately said, going to her bathroom and taking out the lotion. Rubbing it over the girl's feet, she noticed the woman's pedicured toes and smiled, glad that on some level and at some time, someone had taken care of her. She rolled the socks up the girl's legs, smirking as her more oversized clothes hung from the girl's small frame, as Ursula gently dressed her. Picking her up and placing her on the lounge, Ursula took the sheep's skins she kept on the back of the lounge and placed them over the girl's body, her heart-melting when she saw the woman softly smile as the warmth flowed through her body. Just as Ursula was about to get up, the girl's eyes opened once more, this time, able to focus on Ursula. Fear was the first thing she saw in the girl's eyes, and as she reached out to stroke the girl's face, she saw a silent tear roll from her eye.

"You're safe here. I'm not going to let anything bad happen to you now, sweetheart," Ursula lovingly reassured her. The girl's eyes remained fearful, looking around to try and understand her situation. She had been told of these mountain women and their desire for the unnatural. The girl's Mother had never elaborated, merely stating that there was a reason they chose to live alone, without men. She had thought it would be wonderful to live without men, as the only experiences she had had with them had always been cruel, violent, or humiliating. Her Father had offered her to his friends' sons the day she had turned 18, stating that she needed to be wed before her 19th birthday. The one kindness he had shown her, limiting the age of her suitors. They were to be no older than 25. She had known why he had done this. She had been caught looking at the mountain women who would occasionally come down and into the township to buy one thing or the next. The girl was mesmerized the moment she lay eyes on them. Her Mother had seen, coming out of a shop, just as the girl was about to approach one of them, taking her wrist by surprise and slapping her face, just as she had smiled at the woman. Yet now, the girl knew almost instinctively where she was and in whose arms she lay, and she had never felt so close to heaven in her life.

"I," the girl tried to say, her voice cutting out and making Ursula smile kindly.

"You don't have to say anything right now. There'll be plenty of time for talking when you are feeling better," she explained, running her fingers through the girl's soft dry hair and offering her another sip of her tea.

Ursula had watched over the girl for hours after their first encounter. Her color had come back to her face, then her eyes opened for the longest of times, and finally, her voice began to strengthen.

"How long was I out there?" The girl said, surprising Ursula. She had been watching the fire, wondering what horrible creatures had hurt this sweet girl.

"I don't know, but you have made good progress in the few hours you have been here, so

I don't think it was all night. Maybe, sometime early this morning. I'm Ursula. This is Jax," Ursula said, introducing herself and her dog. The girl smiled, Ursula had placed her hand on her stomach, and the girl loved the gentle weight of it. It wasn't the dominating hand of her husband. His touch made her nervous, worried where the next hit would land. This was different. There was a gentleness to this woman's power.

"I'm Kat," Kat replied, craning her neck to look at Jax, who was wagging her tail behind her.

"Jax is lovely," Kat remarked, noticing her shiny well-kept coat. Ursula smiled, hearing Kat's stomach rumble.

"I should go. You've already been so kind to me. I don't want to overstay my welcome," Kat said, making Ursula smile.

"I'd like you to stay. You wouldn't be overstaying your welcome. I think it's been a long time since someone took care of you, if ever, and I'd like to look after you for a little while longer," Ursula replied, deciding that she wouldn't hold back in stating what she wanted. Kat looked at her with her big eyes, a faint smile forming on her young face and the blush of her weeks moistening Ursula's desire.

"I can't argue with that," Kat meekly replied, raising onto her elbows, her toned muscles flexing under Ursula's baggy t-shirt. Ursula smiled, placing an arm under Kat just as her arms gave way, catching Kat and instinctively cradling her against her breast. Ursula paused for a moment, worried that Kat would be repulsed by the action, delighted when Kat left out soft sounds of happiness and buried her face gently into the deep cleavage of Ursula's heavy breasts.

"I've heard the stories of the mountain women. Are they true? Would you rather take the company of women over men?" Kat boldly asked. She was aware that offending her rescuer may have repercussions, but the wetness she felt pooling inside of her was more than she could contain. She wanted to know. She needed to know. If Ursula was one of the women her Mother had warned her about, Kat had already decided that she would let her take her as a man might.

"I cannot speak for every single woman living alone up here. What would you do if I told you that the stories were right, about me at least? Would you be afraid? Tell the authorities?" Ursula questioned, feeling herself fall deep into the mental spaces she loved to feel. Kat tugged at the sheepskins until she was merely laying in Ursula's arms with her only coverings being the baggy clothes she had been dressed in. Kat looked Ursula in the eye before subtly spreading her legs, exposing the softness of her pussy to Ursula's gaze.

"I would have nothing to tell the authorities," Kat replied, surprised when Ursula placed the sheepskins back over her, making her blush. She had thought that Ursula would have taken her right there and then, embarrassed that she had incorrectly read the signs. Yet it was the reassuring pat over her covered pussy, the gentle yet dominant hand that thumped at her, causing her clit to shudder, that confused her.

"I see. Well, I think that we will get on very nicely," Ursula replied, running her hand under Kat's shirt and feeling her skin, just below her smaller breasts, making her gasp. Ursula knew that Kat was on fire for her. She could see it in her pleading eyes. Pleading to be taken, to be used, just as she had been time and time again. Ursula had no intention of continuing Kat's trauma cycle instead of frowning and pulling her hand away.

"You're still cold. Would you let me bathe you?" Ursula asked, keen to see Kat's naked body once more and to continue to warm her from the inside out. Kat simply nodded her head before she felt Ursula's strong arms lifting her in the air and carrying her to the bathroom.

Ursula's renovations meant that the traditional bathroom had been changed to suit a more modern resident. A stone bathtub stood against the floor to ceiling window, and the vanity and toilet were in matching black. The backlight of the panel of the sunken ceiling gave the room a seductive glow, and the shower was three meters of walkthrough, the raindrop showerheads and wall jets creating the perfect combination of massage and comfort. Ursula placed Kat on the extended bench, sitting her up and going to turn the water on. Waiting patiently, Kat looked over Ursula. Her long blonde hair waved with her every movement. Her mountain-woman thighs and large, muscular ass held up her thickset core and large, full breasts. Kat looked at the jeans she wore, the dark denim complimenting the black long sleeve with the deep V cut neckline and fur-lined black leather vest, her breasts highlighted by the under curve the vest emphasized. Ursula turned, catching Kat looking at her lustfully, coming toward her and unzipping her vest, her breasts falling out slightly and bouncing as Ursula knelt before Kat.

"I'm going to help you undress, is that

alright?" She seductively whispered, grabbing a handful of the t-shirt Kat wore and sliding it up slightly, just as Kat nodded her head.

"I need to hear you say it, that it's alright if I undress you," Ursula affectionately instructed. Kat blushed, feeling an unfamiliar sensation of arousal course through her veins.

"Yes, you can undress me," Kat quietly answered, Ursula, making quick work of removing her top.

"It's freezing," Kat involuntarily gasped, worried for a moment that Ursula would be offended at her complaint. Yet, instead of becoming annoyed, Ursula simply smiled and turned up the central heating.

"You'll be warm once we get you in the water," Ursula instructed, hearing the phone ring.

"I'll be right back, darling," Ursula said, turning the water off and heading into the living room where her phone lay on the lounge. Ursula picked it up, her eyebrows raised when she saw the name.

"To what do I owe the pleasure?" Ursula said down the phone. She heard Uda's familiar laugh, her husky tone as sensual as ever.

"We need your help, my lovely friend," Uda said, making Ursula smile. She and Uda had met decades before when Uda and Nikita had passed through her home town. They had spent a marvelous weekend together, barely getting out of bed. Nikita and Uda had never fed on Ursula, respecting her dominant energy and strength, the only human who had ever left both of them speechless.

"I have a few things happening at the moment. If you would be happy to stay in the guest house, you're more than welcome. But I have a fragile little thing staying with me at the moment, and I want to keep her calm. How many girls do you have with you?" Ursula asked. She knew how Uda and Nikita lived and had learned over the years that Uda and Nikita would not be coming alone. The one other thing that was also a well-known fact was that when Uda and Nikita turned up, their stay was never for a mere social visit. Ursula wondered what trouble would arrive at her door and delighted in the adventure.

"Well, it sounds like you have been very busy. Yes, the guest house will be fine. I will explain everything when we see you in a few days," Uda said, hanging up the phone just as Ursula heard a splash coming from the bathroom. Walking quickly back into the bathroom and seeing that Kat had slipped into the bath.

"Why did you think you were strong enough to get yourself in there?" Ursula questioned, looking at Kat's naked body in the water.

"Will you come in with me?" Kat asked, blushing before looking down into the water, afraid to see Ursula's rejection.

"Yes, but not today," Ursula replied, beginning to gently wash Kat's body, rubbing tenderly between her thighs until she heard Kat's involuntarily whimper of desire and surrender.

"I am going to look after you now, baby girl," Ursula whispered into Kat's ear, sending goosebumps over her body.

Chapter 9

Ursula and Kat had spent three days together before Uda and Nikita turned up at their door with the girls in their care. The snow had fallen particularly heavily, and Kat was curled up on the lounge, wrapped in Ursula's heavy coat, rolling the sleeves up as she heard a knock at the door.

"I'll get it. These will be the friends I told you about," Ursula explained, seeing Kat's frightened eyes, happy as they relaxed, and her fear was replaced with anticipation. Ursula walked to the large wooden door, opening it as a gust of freezing wind burst into the house.

"Come in," she said, standing out of the way and inviting Uda and Nikita inside. They silently walked through her door before standing in the entryway, taking off their gloves and scarves.

"I've missed you," Nikita gushed, reaching out and embracing Ursula, the warmth of her womanly body instantly igniting a deep desire within both Nikita and Uda.

"These are our girls, Hannah, Holly, Eden, Kelsey, and Nerada. In no particular order," Uda laughed, introducing her family. Ursula acknowledged each of them before seeing Kat's head above the back of the lounge.

"This is Kat," Ursula said, motioning to the young girl with her raven black hair and piercing green eyes, instantly taking Uda and Nikita's interest.

"And she's mine," Ursula said in a commanding voice, claiming Kat, which made Kat blush and smile.

"And who is this," Kelsey excitedly said, seeing Jax pander toward the group, sitting at Ursula's feet.

"Her name is Jax," Ursula smiled before leading the women through the house and into the guest house. She wanted to get them settled so she could get to the bottom about why they were here.

"You'll find everything you need here. I'll be making dinner in an hour," Ursula said before smiling and leaving.

"You failed to mention how pretty your friends are," Kat said, feeling self-conscious as Ursula re-emerged in the living room and sat down next to her, pulling her to her chest and stroking her hair.

"You don't need to be worried. Those girls are spoken for. Do you remember what I told you about them?" Ursula asked, happy when Kat nodded and snuggled into her before closing her eyes.

"So, how's your Father?" Uda smirked a few hours later as she came into the main house and sat by the fire. Ursula had put a large pot of soup on the stove, and it was simmering fragrantly through the house. Uda and Nikita had killed Ursula's Step Mother and Father years ago. She had always known, if you live by the sword, you die by the sword. She hadn't given it much thought at the time or in the years which followed. There had been no love lost, and it was Ursula's understanding that her Father had put her half-sister in her Mother's sisters care months earlier as he felt the Vampires closing in on him. Ursula had not seen the girl since she was three months old. She hardly felt as though they were family.

Ursula tilted her head and gestured toward the long study table at the front of the house in the library.

"Probably cold this time of year. I can't imagine 6 foot of snow keeps you warm in the ground. Here, I have all the books on the table," Ursula replied, wrapping her arms tighter around Kat.

"Books?" Hannah curiously asked, coming to join them. Kat sat cross-legged in Ursula's lap, enjoying the feeling of being free and yet incredibly possessed. Ursula had a way of giving her every freedom while simultaneously making her feeling beautifully caged and entangled in her.

"Ursula's the daughter of a well-known and rather successful Hunter," Nikita smirked, enjoying the irony of sitting in their enemy's daughter's home. The shock of the revelation hit like waves over the girls as they tried to take in the information they were receiving.

"So, um, can I get a little bit of context?!" Holly dramatically exclaimed, looking around the room, worried about an ambush. Ursula stood up and poured everyone tea, moving around the table before sitting back down and patting Kat to sit on her lap. She waited for her, wrapping an arm around the girl's waist before beginning to speak. This is what Uda and Nikita had always liked about Ursula; she took her time. She was calculating, intense, not one to be rushed or to think with emotion.

"It is true. My Father killed many of their kind. He trained my brothers and me to do the same. And yet, when after my first few kills, it became boring. So I stopped," Ursula explained, holding back the full story much to Uda and Nikita's amusement.

"Did you feel bad for killing them?" Kelsey asked as she sipped her tea. She couldn't imagine how she could ever bring herself to harm Uda or Nikita.

"No. I just thought that it was pointless. I have never had a problem with Vampires, not until I started killing them. I wanted to go back to not having a problem. To live my life, not to live a hunter's life," Ursula added. She looked around the room and smirked at how the girls were so surprised by her story.

"Anyway, just consider me an ally, and we'll get along just fine," Ursula added, reaching out and opening up a thick, leather-bound book. Kat snuggled into her, reading with her and looking at the pictures of the different torture devices the Hunters had used over the centuries. The girls shrugged their shoulders before opening up the various books and going to fine a stop to sit, beginning the research phase of their battle against the Hunters.

***

Over the next three weeks, Ursula's home was transformed from a large yet comfortable log cabin to a hive of survival training. She taught them everything she knew about how the Hunters operate, who their leaders were, and what weaponry they had at their disposal. They also shopped online for the latest covert operations gear, delighting the girls who had taken the first week as a joke.

"We are going to be like spies!" Holly excited exclaimed as she was fitted out with boots, tight pants, and a fitted thermal pullover. Yet the training that Ursula, Uda, and Nikita began to put them through made the fun and games stop rather quickly.

"So, this isn't just an easy shot and run situation?" Kelsey asked as Ursula led them on a mountain run through the snow. Kat had surprised everyone, including herself, with her agility and speed, discovering that being so thin came with its benefits, as she sprinted up the mountainside, barely puffing. Uda and Nikita stayed home, practicing the various types of weapons that they might need to use.

"No. You see, if civilians learn about our world, there will be absolute chaos and all sorts of mayhem," Ursula said as she reached the top lookout and turned around to see where the others were. They focused on fitness conditioning for the last three weeks, every afternoon tackling a new mountain or practicing close combat. After hearing how they tortured and wounded Cleo so severely, Ursula knew that the Hunters were setting up for war. Usually, they would target a rogue Vampire, somebody in a compromised position where they were weakened by their circumstance, but this was not the case. They had chosen to go after two of the most well-known and feared Vampires in the country. Sure, they treated their girls kindly, but Uda and Nikita had a reputation that proceeded them.

"You're all getting much faster," Ursula said, seeing the girls practically file in one after the other. They caught their breath and looked out over the valley to where they could just make out Ursula's home.

"I never thought that I would be going to war. I never thought that I would be training to kill someone. But then I think about how badly Zagan broke my heart, and I'm like, no, I could shoot you in the face," Nerada said, stretching on a rock. Ursula laughed.

"We aren't training you to become killing machines. We want you to be able to run away if you need to slow them down so you can get away and to be able to handle the weapons. Just leave the killing to us," Ursula replied, raising her strong arms above her head in a stretch.

"But if the situation arises, and we need to kill one of them, we can, right? After all, they aren't just going after our Mistresses, they hurt Cleo, and she was human," Hannah stated. Holly raised an eyebrow and nodded her head.

"I suppose, but we are hoping it doesn't come to that. If it does, we will make it look like an accident. The annoying thing about living in two worlds is that you have to obey two sets of rules. It's easier to kill a Vampire than it is with a human," Ursula explained. That was all she wanted to talk about it, signaling to the girls that they should get back to the cabin as the sun rested on the horizon.

"Race you back. The loser has to cook dinner," she said, bolting into a sprint and leaving the girls in her tracks. Ursula made light work of sprinting down the hill for a woman with such a large and strong body, Kat fast on her heels.

Chapter 10

"We've been training for weeks. I don't think I've ever been in such great condition," Holly said, as she stood naked in front of the bathroom mirror. She ran her hands over her stomach, admiring how tight it had become as Uda stepped out of the shower.

"I've noticed," she remarked, digging her fingernails into Holly's breast until she flinched.

"Hmm," Uda said more to herself than to Holly, surprised that Holly pulled away, breaking a rule. Uda smirked, circling Holly before grabbing her by the hair and pulling her to the floor.

"Open your mouth," Uda demanded, lowering herself onto Holly's mouth and grinding into her. Holly obediently licked and sucked Uda's pussy, feeling her legs spread as Nikita entered the room.

"I can't believe you started without me," she said, pushing an 8inch dildo into Holly, making her scream into Uda's cunt.

"Yes, make her do that again," Uda moaned as Nikita began to fuck her, causing her to moan over and over into Uda. The night before, the members of their coven were to arrive, and they wanted to make the most of the privacy while they still had it.

Their moans could be heard from the other end of the house as Ursula, and the other girls ate dinner.

"So," Eden said, laughing and trying to break the silence at the table.

"How long have you know Uda and Nikita?" Hannah asked. As the weeks had passed, it was clear that Ursula, Uda, and Nikita had a long and loyal history.

Ursula had been pleasantly surprised at how calm Kat at been when she had told her who Uda and Nikita were, but she wasn't sure that she was ready for this next story.

"Well. It's a long story," Ursula said as she heard Nikita.

"I think we've got time," Kat laughed, squeezing Ursula's hand. Smiling, Ursula finished her beer before gesturing for the group to move to the lounges by the fire.

"I've told you that my father was Hunter. What I didn't tell you was how we fell out. I was young and fell in love with a woman who just so happened to be a Vampire. She was a member of Uda and Nikita's coven. When my father found out, he made it his mission to hunt her down and kill her. Which he did, right in front of my eyes. From that day forward, I stopped talking to him or my brothers. The last time I heard, only one of my brothers is still alive. That's what I meant when I said I didn't want a Hunter's life. They don't tend to live particularly long. Anyway, when Nessie was murdered, Uda and Nikita turned the tables and began to hunt my father, wanting to kill him as revenge," Ursula explained.

"Which we did, with your help," Uda said, coming into the space and sitting down, collapsing in an armchair.

"You helped kill your father?" Eden asked. She couldn't help but feel close to Ursula, hoping that the rest of the story wasn't the story she knew all too well.

"Yes. He had left my mother and remarried. They had a daughter together. We wanted until he had sent his daughter to her mother's family before I told them where he would be, but the plan didn't go to plan," Ursula said, cracking her neck and looking at Nikita, who had joined Uda on the armchair.

"Only he was meant to be there, but his wife had come home early. So, we killed her before we turned on him. We chained him to the wall and lit the house of fire. He was meant to die, but that man, some people just don't want to die. He escaped and had been a crazy homeless person until recently. The Order has him and is going to make an example of him to the other

Hunters. He is an inspiration to them, Heidi plans to hold a huge convention, and his death will be the highlight of the evening. He hunted and killed over half our coven before he killed Nessie," Nikita explained. Eden's stomach was knotted. This was her family they were talking about, which meant that Ursula was her half-sister, and Uda, Nikita, and Ursula had been the reason that her mother had died, and her father had become an alcoholic.

"Fuck, hectic," Eden sighed, getting up and walking into the kitchen to get a beer.

What the fuck, Eden thought to herself, unsure how to feel, yet feeling more overwhelmed than she had ever felt in her life. Deciding that she would go to bed, Eden excused herself and made her way to her room. She lay on top of the made bed and let the tears pour down her cheeks. She knew that Nikita and Uda could read minds, but she didn't care. If they bothered to tap into her mind, what could she even do to stop it? So she let the thoughts flow.

They killed my parents. Sure, my dad made it out, but he was never the same. He died that day too. Do they know? Is that why they let me into their world?! Eden thought angrily to herself as she took the diamond bracelet Nikita had recently bought her and threw it against the wall, breaking it before she turned onto her stomach and screamed into the mattress.

Did you hear that? Nikita asked Uda, looking at her and acting as though this wasn't the biggest inconvenience.

Yes. How could I miss it? She is screaming at us right now, Uda replied.

I don't think Ursula even knows that Eden's her sister, probably because Eden isn't her real name, Nikita replied, looking over at Ursula. The latter was talking intimately at Kat as they cuddled in front of the fire.

What. The. Actual. Fuck. What are we going to do now? Nikita asked.

Well, we could talk to her, maybe she will forgive us? Uda suggested, knowing that Eden would not let this go.

I don't think that's going to happen. She had to go, one way or the other, Nikita declared.

I don't want to kill her. If Ursula ever finds out, she might turn on us. And I don't want that to happen. She knows far too much about our culture and society. She would be a threat that would destroy us, Uda said, standing up and yawning.

"I'm going to go to bed too," Uda said, holding out her hand to Nikita, who took it eagerly.

"Night," Nikita said, walking down towards Eden's room.

Opening the door, they saw Eden crying on the bedspread.

"Eden. We didn't know," Nikita lovingly said. She was genuinely saddened that Eden was hurting so intensely. Eden sat up. Her face was red and puffy.

"I get it. But I wasn't at my grandparent's house. I was there. I saw you two do it. I just didn't know that it was you when I saw you again. I didn't know anything!" Eden yelled as loudly as she could. Uda slammed the door shut as she heard Ursula and the other girls stand up and begin to make their way to Eden's room to see what the commotion was.

"Get the fuck out!" Eden yelled, throwing a pillow at Nikita. She and Uda looked at each other before the door burst open, and Ursula and the other girls walked in.

"What the fuck is going on?" Ursula said, annoyed that Eden's dramatics was ruining their enjoyable evening.

"Are you going to tell her, or should I?" Uda asked Eden, who was glaring at her.

"Tell me what?" Ursula said, coming to sit on the bed next to Eden. She had felt it too, the strange pull towards the girl.

"You're sisters," Nikita said, deciding that it was better to air this out now, once and for all.

"What?" Ursula scoffed. Eden sat up and crossed her legs before looking at Ursula.

"How old are you? My sister wasn't called Eden. Her name is," Ursula said, stopping when Eden interrupted her.

"Amanda," Eden said, causing Ursula's eyes to go wide, fearful that Uda and Nikita had played a trick on her.

"What's this all about? You come into my home just to drop this bombshell on me?" Ursula growled, pushing Uda against the wall, taking her by surprise. She was not the only one who was surprised, as Uda took a moment before fighting back.

"No, we have enough going on. We don't have time for games, and we certainly do not have time for this," Uda said, pushing Ursula's hands off her. Eden got up, walked over to Nikita, and tried to punch her in the face, getting her fist blocked by Uda's hand.

"I know you are upset, but you don't want to start a fight with us," Uda calmly said, pushing Eden back.

"You're going to need to start from the

beginning," Ursula said, reaching out and pulling on Eden's hand.

"Don't touch me. You're just as bad as they are. You led them to my parents. My Mom died because of you," Eden said, slapping at Ursula until she let her go. Eden ran to the door, down the stairs, and toward the cars, grabbing Uda's keys on the way out before slamming the door shut with all her might.

"Well, that went well," Nikita said, slumping down on the bed next to Ursula.

"Oh, don't look at me like that. I had no idea she was his daughter," she groaned, annoyed that there was a new drama which would need to be solved.

"I want to go after her, but I don't see much point. She's so angry right now. Let's just refocus on what we have to prepare, and when she comes back, we can discuss everything then," Ursula said before sighing heavily and standing up.

"Let's go. We have to make up our kits

and put them in our hiding spots," Ursula said, running her fingers through her long hair, grabbing Kat's hand on the way out of the room, and leaving Uda and Nikita sitting alone in silence.

***

Eden drove like a madwoman, uninterested in the road rules of the human world. She followed the road, winding down the mountains, wiping the tears from her eyes. She was grateful that nobody had followed her. She wanted to be alone. She needed it.

Driving into a small town, she pulled into a street park and turned off the ignition, sitting in silence in the luxury car. She felt numb. She had had her suspicions that it had been Uda and Nikita who had killed her mother and broken her father, yet having that theory confirmed had made her sick to her stomach.

I've fucked them. I've let them feed on me.

My half-sister was the one who led them to my parents, to me, Eden thought. She let the tears pour from her eyes, the stinging saltiness rolling onto her lips and making her heart heavy. Getting out of the car, she blinked a few times to clear her eyes, locking the car and walking into the closest café. Sitting down, she was immediately joined by Heidi, much to Eden's displeasure.

"What the fuck do you want?!" Eden practically yelled, taking Heidi by surprise and causing the other patrons in the café to turn and look at the two of them.

"That's no way to speak to me," Heidi replied, the amusement in her eye telling Eden that she was not offended. Eden took a menu from the waitress, but Heidi politely declined.

"What do you want, Heidi?" Eden asked. Her voice was filled with emotional exhaustion, enough to grab Heidi's attention.

"I don't usually answer human's questions. But you're not just any human, are you?" Heidi replied.

"What are you talking about?" Eden asked as her blueberry pancakes were placed in front of her.

"I know your father," Heidi said, making Eden roll her eyes.

"I know you do. You have him trapped somewhere. You're going to have a convention and kill him in front of everyone," Eden said, stabbing into her blueberries. Heidi laughed a laugh, which caused Eden to hold up her knife and point it at her.

"What the fuck is so funny?!" Eden interrogated. Heidi became very serious, more serious than she had ever seen Uda or Nikita.

"I'm glad they told you about the event. It is true. I do have your father. But he is not trapped. He is living quite well. And I am holding a convention. But he won't die," Heidi explained, as Eden's eyes became bigger and bigger.

"What do you mean? They said," Eden said, getting cut off.

"They told you the lie I told them. What is going to happen is all those who follow and support Uda and Nikita will be killed by the army of Hunters I have coming to the event. Your father is just the lure to get them and all their supporters in one place," Heidi explained, taking Eden by surprise.

"But now that I've told you that. I can't very well leave you to go back to them and tell them the real reason I will hold the conference," Heidi said, reaching over and clutching Eden's wrist.

"So this is what we are going to do. You're going to come with me, and you can stay with your father. It's been a long time since you've seen him from what he has been telling me," Heidi said, paying for Eden's pancakes and pulling her to her feet.

"Why are you so nice to me? I heard what you did to Hannah. I saw the marks you scared into her skin," Eden questioned, causing Heidi to roll her eyes.

"I'm not *nice*. I will come for what I want, and you'll give it to me one way or another, but right now, I see no need to go down that path. Would you like to see your father?" Heidi said, causing Eden's head to spin. Nodding, she stood almost involuntarily and followed Heidi outside. The clouds which hung overhead allowed Heidi to move through the town with ease. Holding the door to her car open for Eden, Eden slowly got in, looking back at Uda's car parked outside the café.

Fuck those bitches, Eden angrily thought as she felt the car door close and watched Heidi walk around to the driver's side.

"Ready?" Heidi asked, her fire-red hair tussling around her shoulders, her green eyes seducing Eden faster than Uda or Nikita ever had.

"Yeah," Eden whispered, blushing and pulling her knees up to her chest. Heidi slowly pushed Eden's knees down, her feet landing back on the floor. Heidi's hand slid up Eden's thighs and gently parted them, enjoying the warmth that greeted her.

"Good girl," Heidi whispered, her eyes locking onto Eden's and holding the gaze until she saw Eden's submission. Smiling to herself in satisfaction at how easy it was to tear Eden away from Uda and Nikita, Heidi began to drive out of the car space and onto the road.

"This will be easier than I first thought," Heidi announced as she strolled into the room filled with old men, seductively eyeing Zagan as Eden followed closely behind.

"I am surprised you've brought her here. You've taken a huge risk. Uda and Nikita and those who follow them could be surrounding us at the very moment. They will come for her," Zagan growled, annoyed that Heidi controlled the current turn of events. Heidi and the Hunters had agreed. They would hunt Uda, Nikita, and their followers within the coven to eliminate anyone who threatened Heidi's rule, control, and power. It always came back to power and control, and Uda and Nikita commanded it without even trying. The only reason they weren't the Queen of the coven was that they passed on it when it was offered to them. Heidi had been the coven's second choice, and even after 300 years, she couldn't let it go. Whenever there had been a serious discussion or decision, Uda and Nikita had the final say, with their supports outnumbering Heidi's, and Heidi was not interested in her authority being undermined another moment longer. When Uda and Nikita had taken a softer approach to feeding, although the coven made jokes, no one dared seriously question them. Heidi had never had that kind of power and had to work tirelessly to convince and persuade, manipulate, and threaten to move forward with the simplest of plans.

"That is the intention. They will come for her, and I mean, who could blame them. And when they come, you will already be ready. I have served them to you on a silver platter. You should be thanking me," Heidi replied, running her nails down Zagan's cheek. He aggressively pulled away from her and sat down in disgust that he secretly was turned on by the seductress.

"Once you have them. I decide who you hunt. That is the agreement," Heidi declared to the group, reminding them that it is in everyone's best interests to continue to work together.

"Well, where are they then?" A man sitting next to the burning fire in the fireplace asked. Heidi handed Eden a phone, Eden silently dialing a number and putting the phone on loudspeaker.

"Hello?" Came Uda's voice down the phone. The men in the room began to turn toward each other.

"Uda?" Eden replied, the pretend fear in her voice, making Heidi smile.

"Eden!" Uda exclaimed.

"Where are you? You've been gone for days. We found my car in town. Are you alright?!" Uda said, Nikita coming to the phone, Uda having put it on loudspeaker.

"I'm so sorry it went that way, Eden. Where are you? We are coming to get you," Nikita said, the relief in her voice making Eden's stomach churn, causing her to feel guilty about the trap she was about to lead them into.

"I'm with Heidi, she saw me at a café in town and forced me to go with her. We are somewhere on the edge of town, on the other side from where my sis, from where Ursula's home is. I have to go, please, get me. I don't want to be here with her. She hurts me," Eden said, tearing up and crying down the phone. She knew that Uda and Nikita would be enraged that Heidi had taken her, their heightened anger in their response evidence of their affection.

"Eden, hold on," Nikita said, Heidi, taking the phone and ending the call, smiling sinisterly at Eden, catching the slightest feeling of regret in her eyes before turning to the men.

"I don't know what you are all still doing

here. The coven will come with a force to be reckoned within roughly 16 hours. I would prepare if I were you," Heidi said, placing her hand on the back of Eden's neck and squeezing until Eden whimpered and tried to pull away.

"And now, let's have some fun," Heidi whispered in Eden's ear, running her fingers through the girl's hair as the men left the room, Heidi closing the doors slowly behind them and locking the door.

To be continued